Mel's hand was enclosed in his and she was standing close to him now.

So close that, if she pressed forward, she would bind herself against the strong column of his body. She longed to feel that sheathed, muscled strength against the pliant wand of her own body, to lift her mouth to his and wind her fingers up into the base of his neck and draw that sculpted mouth down upon hers...

It shook her, the intensity of the urge to do so. Like a slow-motion film running inside her head, she felt her brain try to reason her way out of it. Out of the urge to reach for him, to kiss him...

It had been so, so long since she had kissed a man, any man at all. And longer still since she had given reign to the physical impulse of intimacy. And now here she was, gazing up at a man who was the most achingly seductive she'd ever encountered, wanting only to feel his mouth on hers, his arms around her. As if he heard her body call to him, Nikos's mouth, as he bent his head to catch her lips, was as soft as velvet. As sensuous as silk.

Dissolving her completely.

Julia James lives in England and adores the peaceful, verdant countryside and the wild shores of Cornwall. She also loves the Mediterranean, so rich in myth and history, its sun-baked landscape and olive groves, ancient ruins and azure seas. "The perfect setting for romance—rivaled only by the lush tropic heat of the Caribbean. Palms swaying by a silver sand beach lapped by turquoise waters...what more could lovers want?"

Books by Julia James

Harlequin Presents®

The Forbidden Touch of Sanguardo
Securing the Greek's Legacy
Painted the Other Woman
The Dark Side of Desire
The Theotokis Inheritance
From Dirt to Diamonds
Buttoned-Up Secretary, British Boss
Forbidden or For Bedding?
The Master of Highbridge Manor
Penniless and Purchased
The Boselli Bride
The Playboy of Pengarroth Hall
The British Billionaire's Innocent
The Greek's Million-Dollar Baby Bargain

Visit the Author Profile page
at Harlequin.com for more titles.

Julia James

—

Captivated by the Greek

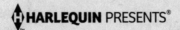
HARLEQUIN PRESENTS®

ISBN-13: 978-0-373-13365-9

Captivated by the Greek

First North American publication 2015

Copyright © 2015 by Julia James

Recycling programs for this product may not exist in your area.

Printed in U.S.A.

www.Harlequin.com

Captivated by the Greek

For carers everywhere—you are all saints!

CHAPTER ONE

NIKOS PARAKIS TWISTED his wrist slightly to glance at his watch and frowned. If he wanted to make his appointment in the City he was going to have to skip lunch. No way could he fit in a midday meal now, having delayed leaving his Holland Park apartment—his base in the UK—in order to catch a lengthy teleconference with Russian clients. He'd also, on this early summer's day, wanted to get some fresh air and brief exercise, so had dismissed his driver and intended to pick up a taxi on the far side of the park, in Kensington High Street.

As he gained the wide tree-lined pavement he felt a stab of hunger. He definitely needed refuelling.

On impulse, he plunged across the road and headed for what appeared to be some kind of takeaway food shop. He was no food snob, despite the wealth of the Parakis banking dynasty at his disposal, and a sandwich was a sandwich—wherever it came from.

The moment he stepped inside, however, he almost changed his mind. Fast food outlets specialising in pre-packed sandwiches had come a long way in thirty years, but this was one of the old-fashioned ones where sandwiches were handmade on the spot, to order, constructed out of the array of ingredients contained in plastic tubs behind the counter.

Damn, he thought, irritated, he really didn't have time for this.

But he was here now, and it would have to do.

'Have you anything ready-made?' he asked, addressing the person behind the counter. He didn't mean to sound brusque, but he was hungry and in a hurry.

The server, who had her back to him, went on buttering a slice of bread. Nikos felt irritation kick again.

'She's making mine first, mate,' said a voice nearby, and he saw that there was a shabbily dressed, grizzled-looking old man seated on a chair by the chilled drinks cabinet. 'You'll 'ave ter wait.'

Nikos's mouth pressed tight, and he moved his annoyed regard back to the figure behind the counter. Without turning, the server spoke.

'Be with you in a sec,' she said, apparently to Nikos, and started to pile ham onto the buttered slice before wrapping the sandwich in a paper serviette and turning to hand it to the man. She pushed a cup of milky tea towards him, too.

'Ta, luv,' the man said, moving to stand closer to Nikos than he felt entirely comfortable with.

Whenever the man had last bathed, it hadn't been recently. Nor had he shaved. Moreover, there was a discernible smell of stale alcohol about him.

The man closed grimy fingers around the wrapped sandwich, picked up the mug in a shaky grip and looked at Nikos.

'Any spare change, guv?' he asked hopefully.

'No,' said Nikos, and turned back to the server, who was now wiping the sandwich preparation surface clean.

The old man shuffled out.

The server's voice followed him. 'Stay off the booze, Joe—it's killing you.'

'Any day now, luv, any day…' the man assured her.

He shuffled out and was gone, lunch provided. Presumably for free, Nikos supposed, having seen no money change hands for the transaction. But his interest in the matter was zero, and with the server finally free to pay him attention, he repeated his original question about the availability of ready-made sandwiches—this time most definitely impatiently.

'No,' replied the server, turning around and busying herself with the tea urn.

Her tone of voice had changed. If Nikos could have been bothered to care—which he didn't, in the slightest—he might have said she sounded annoyed.

'Then whatever's quickest.'

He glanced at his watch again, and frowned. This was ridiculous—he was wasting time instead of saving it!

'What would you like?'

The server's pointless question made his frown deepen.

'I said whatever's quickest,' he repeated.

'That,' came the reply, 'would be bread and butter.'

Nikos dropped his wrist and levelled his gaze right at her. There was no mistaking the antagonism in her tone. Or the open irritation in his as he answered.

'Ham,' he bit out.

'On white or brown? Baguette or sliced?'

'Whatever's quickest.' How many times did he have to *say* that?

'That would be white sliced.'

'White sliced, then.'

'Just ham?'

'Yes.' Anything more complicated and he'd be there all day.

She turned away and busied herself at the preparation surface behind her. Nikos drummed his fingers on the counter. Realising he was thirsty, he twisted round to help himself to a bottle of mineral water from the chilled drinks cabinet against the wall.

As he put it on the counter the server turned round, sandwich prepared and wrapped in a paper serviette. She glanced at the bottle and Nikos could see she was mentally calculating the combined price.

'Three pounds forty-five,' she said.

He had his wallet out already, taking out a note.

'That's a *fifty*,' she said, as if she'd never seen one before.

Perhaps she never had, thought Nikos acidly. He said nothing, just went on holding it out for her.

'Haven't you anything smaller?' she demanded.

'No.'

With a rasp of irritation she snatched it from him and opened the till. There was some audible clinking and rustling, and a moment later she was clunking his change down on the countertop. It consisted of silver to make it up to a fiver, a single twenty-pound note and twenty-five individual pound coins.

Then she raised her gaze to Nikos and glared at him.

And for the first time Nikos looked at her.

Looked at her—and *saw* her.

He stilled completely. Somewhere inside his head a voice was telling him to stop staring, to pick up the ludicrous heap of coins and pocket the note and get the hell out of there. Get a taxi, get to his meeting, get on with the rest of his life and forget he'd ever been hungry enough to step into some two-bit sandwich bar patronised by alcoholic down-and-outs.

But the voice went totally and entirely unheeded.

Right now only one part of his brain was functioning. The part that was firing in instant, total intensity with the most visceral masculine response he had ever experienced in his life.

Thee mou, but she was absolutely beautiful.

There was no other word for her. In an instant Nikos took in a face that was sculpted to perfection: high cheekbones, contoured jawline, straight nose not a millimetre too long or too short, wide-set eyes of startling blue, and a mouth... Ah, a mouth whose natural lushness was as inviting as a honey-drenched dessert...

How the hell didn't I notice her straight away?

But the question searing through him was irrelevant. Everything right now was irrelevant except his desire—his need—to keep drinking her in. Taking in the incredible impact her stunning looks were having on him. His eyes narrowed in their instinctive, potent perusal of her features, and he felt his response course through him.

He was not a man who had been deprived of the company of beautiful women in his thirty-odd years. As the heir to the Parakis banking dynasty he'd become accustomed to having the hottest girls making a beeline for him. And he knew that it wasn't just the Parakis millions that drew them in. Nature, for whatever capricious reason, had bestowed upon him a six-foot frame—which he kept in peak condition with rigorous and ruthless physical exercise—and looks that, without vanity, he knew women liked. Liked a lot.

The combination had proved highly successful, and his private life was plentifully supplied by any number of keen and eager females only too happy to be seen on his arm, or to keep him company in bed. Given that, therefore, it would have been perverse of him not to have chosen those females who were of the very highest calibre when it came to their appearance.

And this woman, who had drawn his attention so rivetingly, was most definitely of that elite calibre.

His gaze worked over her, and as it did so another realisation struck him. She wasn't wearing a trace of make-up and her hair—blonde, from what little he could see of it—was concealed under some kind of baseball cap. As for her figure—although she appeared to be tall—she was clad in a baggy T-shirt that bore the legend 'Sarrie's Sarnies' and did less than nothing for her.

Hell, if she looked this good stuck in this dump, dressed in grunge, what would she look like dressed in designer labels?

For a moment—just a moment—he felt an overriding desire to put that to the test.

Then, in the next second, he crashed and burned.

'If you want a piece of meat, try a butcher's shop!'

The server's harsh voice cut right through Nikos's riveted attention to her physical attributes.

A frown of incomprehension—and annoyance—pulled his brows together.

'What?' he demanded.

Her face was set. Absently Nikos noted how looking angry actually made her even more stunning. Her cerulean eyes flashed like sapphires.

'Don't give me that,' she snapped. 'Now, take your change, *and* your damn sandwich, and go!'

It was Nikos's turn to experience anger. His face hardened. 'Your rudeness to a customer,' he said freezingly, 'is totally unacceptable. Were you one of *my* employees you would be dismissed instantly for taking such an attitude to those whose custom pays your wages.'

For answer, she put the palms of her hands on the counter—Nikos found himself noting how well shaped they were—and braced herself.

'And if I worked for *you*—which, thank God, I don't—I would be suing *you* for sexual harassment!' she bit back. Her eyes narrowed to slits. '*That's* what I meant by wanting "meat", sunshine!'

Nikos's expression changed. The hardness was still in his eyes, but there was something else, too. A glint that, had the stunning but inexplicably bolshie female facing him been one of his acquaintances, she would have known sent a crystal-clear message.

'Since when is it illegal to admire a woman's beauty?' he riposted silkily.

To prove his point he let his gaze wash over her again. Inside him, the visceral reaction she'd aroused so powerfully warred with the irritation he'd felt ever since his hunger had hit him—an irritation that her hostility and rudeness had elevated to outright anger. He wasn't sure which emotion was predominant. What he *was* sure of, though, was that right now his overpowering desire was to rattle her cage...

'If you *want* to go round ogling women like *meat*, then you should damn well wear sunglasses and spare us the ordeal,' she shot back.

Nikos felt yet another emotion spark through him. Almost unconsciously, he found himself starting to enjoy himself.

One arched eyebrow quirked tauntingly. 'Ordeal?' he asked limpidly.

And then, quite deliberately, he let his gaze soften. No longer assessing. More...caressing. Letting her see clearly that women who received his approbation most definitely did not regard it as an *ordeal*...

And before his eyes, to his intense satisfaction, he saw a wave of colour suffuse her clear, translucent skin. Her cheeks grew stained and her gaze dropped.

'Go away,' she said. Her voice was tight. 'Just...*go away*!'

He gave a low laugh. *Game, set and match—thank you very much.* He didn't need any further confirmation to know that he'd just effortlessly breached her defences...got right past that bolshie anger barrier and hit home, sweet home.

With a sweeping gesture he scooped the pile of coins into his pocket, together with the solitary twenty-pound note, then picked up his ham sandwich and the bottle of water.

'Have a nice day,' he said flippantly, and strolled out of the sandwich shop.

His irritation was gone completely.

As he emerged he saw the down-and-out, Joe, leaning against a nearby lamppost, wolfing down the sandwich he had been given. On impulse, Nikos reached into his jacket pocket, jingling with all the pound coins she'd landed him with.

He scooped up a handful and proffered them. 'You asked about spare change,' he said to the man, who was eyeing him.

'Ta, guv,' said the man, and took the handful eagerly, his bloodshot eyes gleaming.

His grimy hands were shaking, and Nikos felt a pang of pity go through him.

'She's right, you know,' he heard himself telling the man. 'The booze *is* killing you.'

The bloodshot eyes met his. They were not gleaming now. There was desolation in them.

'I know, mate...'

He pulled his gaze away and then he was off again, shuffling down the street, pocketing the money, shoulders hunched in defeat. For a moment Nikos's eyes stayed on him. Then he saw a taxi cab approaching along the High Street, with its 'For Hire' sign illuminated. He flagged it down and flung himself into the back seat, starting to wolf down his ham sandwich.

His own words to the down-and-out echoed in his head. *'She's right, you know...'*

His jaw tightened. Damn—she was, too. And not just about that wretched alcoholic.

Finishing his sandwich, he lifted his mobile phone from his inside pocket and pressed the speed-dial key for his London PA. She answered immediately, and Nikos gave her his instructions.

'Janine, I need to have some flowers delivered...'

Mel stood, palms still pressed into the surface of the counter, and glared after the tall retreating figure. She was mad—totally hopping mad. She hadn't been this angry since she couldn't remember when.

Damn the arrogance of the man!

She could feel her jaw still clenching. She hadn't liked him the moment he'd walked into the shop. The way he'd spoken—not even waiting for her to turn around to him, just making his demands as if she was some kind of servant. Underling. Minion. *Lackey.* The insulting words marched through her head.

She'd tried for her customary politeness while she was finishing Joe's sandwich, but then she'd caught the way the damn man had looked at Joe—as if he was a bad smell. Well, yes, he was—but that wasn't the point. The point was that Joe was in a bad way, and for heaven's sake *anyone* would have felt pity for the guy, surely? Especially—and now her jaw clenched even more—especially a man whom life had so obviously *not* treated anything *like* as grimly as it had poor old Joe.

That had put her back up straight away. And from then on it had just got worse.

The whole monosyllabic exchange about what kind of sandwich he'd wanted replayed itself in her head, followed by—oh yes—his dropping a fifty-pound note down in payment. Mel's mouth tightened in satisfaction. Well, it had given her particular pleasure to dump all those pound coins on him by way of change.

Boy, it had riled him—she had seen that immediately. Trouble was…and now her expression changed yet again, to a mix of anger and something else quite entirely…he had had that comeback on her…

Right through her body she could feel the heat flush. It was running right through her—through every vein, right out to the tips of her fingers—as though someone has tipped hot water into her. And to her own mortification she even felt glorious heat pooling in her core, felt her breasts start to tingle with traitorous reaction.

Oh, damn! Damn, damn, damn!

Yet she couldn't stop herself. Couldn't stop the memory—instant, vivid and overpowering—of the way he'd looked at her. Looked *right* at her. Looked her over…

Meat, she said desperately to herself. *As if you were a piece of meat—that's how he looked at you. Just as you told him.*

She fought to call back the burst of satisfaction she'd felt when she'd rapped that out at him, but it was impossible. All that was possible now was to go on feeling the wonderful flush of heat coursing through her. She fought it down as best she could, willing it to leave her—to leave her alone—just as she'd told him to go, just *go away*...

She shut her eyes, sighing heavily—hopelessly. *OK— OK*, she reasoned, *so face it*. However rude, arrogant and obnoxious he was, he was also—yup, she had to admit it—absolutely, totally and completely drop-dead *devastating*.

She'd registered it instantly—it would have been impossible not to—the minute she'd turned round with Joe's sandwich to see just who it was who'd spoken to her in such a brusque, demanding fashion. Registered it, but had promptly busied herself in making Joe's tea, pinning her eyes on pouring it out and ladling sugar into it the way Joe needed it.

But she'd been conscious of that first glimpse of Mr Drop-dead Devastating burning a hole in her retina— burning its way into her brain—so that all she'd wanted to do was lift her gaze and let it do what it had been trying to do with an urgency she still bewailed and berated.

Which was simply to stare and stare and stare...

At *everything* about him.

His height...his lean, fit body, sheathed in that hand-tailored suit that had fitted him like a glove, reaching across wide shoulders and moulding his broad chest just as the expanse of pristine white shirt had.

But it wasn't his designer suit or even his lean physique that was dominating her senses now.

It was his eyes. Eyes that were night-dark and like tempered steel in a face that was constructed in some particular way that outdid every male she'd ever seen— on-screen or off. Chiselled jaw, strong nose, tough-looking cheekbones, winged brows and always, *always*, those ludicrously long-lashed, gold-flecked eyes that were lethal weapons entirely on their own.

That was what she'd wanted to gaze at, and that was what had been searing through her head all through their snarling exchange.

And then, as if a switch had been thrown, he'd suddenly changed the subject…

More heat coursed through her as the physical memory of how he'd looked at her hit her again. Turning the blatant focus of his male reaction on her like a laser beam. One that had burned right through her.

The slow wash of his gaze had poured over her like warm, molten honey—like a silken touch to her skin. It had felt as though he were caressing her, as if she could actually feel his hands shaping her body, his mouth lowering to hers to taste, to tease…to arouse.

All that in a single sensual glance…

And then, when she'd been helpless—pathetically, abjectly helpless—to do anything other than tell him—beg him—to leave, what had he done? He'd *laughed*! Laughed at her—knowing perfectly well how he'd got the better of her, how he'd made a cringing mockery of her defiance.

The colour in her cheeks turned to hectic spots as anger burned out that shaming blush he'd conjured in her.

Damn him!

Fuming, she went on staring blindly out through the shop door. She could no longer see him. With a final damning adjuration to herself to stop thinking of him, and everything about him, she whirled around to get on with her work.

Washing up had never been so noisy, nor slicing bread so vicious.

CHAPTER TWO

'DID YOU HAVE those flowers delivered?'

It was the first question Nikos found himself asking as he returned to his London office after his meeting that afternoon. He did not doubt that his PA had complied, for she was efficiency itself—and she was used to despatching flowers to the numerous assorted females that featured in his life when he was in the UK.

But not usually to females who worked in sandwich bars...

Mouthy, contrary females who gave him a hard time...

Possessed of looks so stunning he still could not get them out of his head...

He gave a shake of his head, clearing the memory and settling himself down at his desk. There really was no point thinking about the blonde any more. Let alone speculating, as he found himself wanting to do, on just what she might look like if she were dressed in an outfit that adorned her extraordinary beauty.

How much more beautiful could she look?

The question rippled through his mind, and in its wake came a ripple of something that was not idle speculation but desire...

With her hair loosened, a gown draping her slen-

*der yet rounded figure, her sapphire eyes luminous
and long-lashed...*

He cut the image. She'd been a fleeting fiery encounter and nothing more.

No, he thought decisively, switching on his PC, he'd sent flowers to atone for his rudeness—provoking though *she'd* been—and he would leave it at that. He had women enough to choose from—no need to add another one.

He flicked open his diary to see what was coming up in the remainder of his sojourn in London. His father, chairman of the family-run Athens-based investment bank, left that city reluctantly these days, and Nikos found himself doing nearly all the foreign travel that running the bank required.

A frown moved fleetingly across his brow. At least here in London he was spared his father's wandering into the office to make one of his habitual complaints about Nikos's mother. The moment Nikos got back to Athens, though, he knew there would be a litany of complaints awaiting him, while his father indulged himself and offloaded. Then—predictably—the next time he saw his mother a reciprocal litany would be pressed upon him...

With a sigh of exasperation he pushed his interminably warring parents out of his head space. There was never going to be an end to their virulent verbal attacks on each other, their incessant sniping and backbiting. It had gone on for as long as Nikos could remember, and he was more than fed up with it.

Briskly, he ran an eye down the diary page and then frowned again—for quite a different reason this time.
Damn.

His frown deepened. How had he got himself involved in *that*? A black-tie charity bash at the Viscari St James Hotel this coming Friday evening.

In itself, that would not have been a problem. What *was* a problem, though, was that he could see from the diary that the evening included Fiona Pellingham. Right now that woman was *not* someone he wanted to encounter.

A high-flying mergers-and-acquisitions expert at a leading business consultancy, Fiona had taken an obvious shine to Nikos during a business meeting on his last visit to London, and had made it strikingly clear to him that she'd very much like to make an acquisition of *him* for herself.

But for all her striking brunette looks and svelte figure she was, as Nikos had immediately realised, the possessive type, and she would want a great deal more from him than the passing affair that was all he ever indulged in when it came to women. And that meant that the last thing he wanted to do was to give her an opportunity to pursue her obvious interest in him.

He frowned again. The problem was, even if he didn't go to this charity bash she'd somehow put into his diary, Fiona would probably find another way to pursue him. Plague him with yet more invitations and excuses to meet up with him. What he needed was to put her off completely. Convince her he was unavailable romantically.

What he needed was a handy, convenient female he could take along with him on Friday to keep Fiona at bay. But just who would fit that bill? For a moment his mind was totally, absolutely blank. Then, in the proverbial light-bulb moment, he knew exactly who he wanted to take. And the knowledge made him sit back abruptly and hear the question shaping itself inside his head.

*Well, after all, why not? You did want to know just
how much more beautiful she could look if she were
dressed for the evening...*

This would be a chance to find out—why not take it?

A slow smile started to curve his mouth.

Mel was staring at the cluttered table in the back room
behind the sandwich bar. She didn't see the clutter—all
she saw was the huge bouquet that sat in its own cellophane container of water, its opulent blooms as large
as her fists. A bouquet that was so over-the-top it was
ridiculous. Her eyes were stormy.

Who the hell did he think he was?

Except that she knew the answer to that, because his
name came at the end of the message on the card in the
envelope pinned to the cellophane.

Hope these make amends and improve your mood.

It was signed 'Nikos Parakis.'

Her brows lowered. So he was Greek. It made sense,
now she thought about it, because although his English
accent had been perfect, his clipped public-school vow-
els a perfect match with the rest of his 'Mr Rich' look,
nevertheless his complexion had a distinctly Mediterranean hue to it, and his hair was as dark as a raven's
wing.

Even as she thought about it his image sprang into
her vision again—and with it the expression in those
dark, long-lashed eyes that had looked her over, assessing her, clearly liking what he saw...

As if he was finding me worthy of his attentions!

She bristled all over again, fulminating as she glared
at the hapless bouquet of lilies. Their heady scent filled

the small space, obliterating the smell of food that always permeated the room from the sandwich bar beyond. The scent made her feel light-headed. Its strength was almost overpowering, sending coils of fragrance into her lungs. Exotic, perfumed...sensuous.

As sensuous as his gaze had been.

That betraying heat started to flush up inside her again, and with a growl of anger at her own imbecility she wheeled about. She had no idea where she was going to put the ridiculously over-the-top bouquet, but right now she had work to do.

She was manning the sandwich bar on her own because Sarrie himself was on holiday. She didn't mind because he was paying her extra, and every penny was bankable.

As she returned to her post behind the counter, checking what was left of the day's ingredients and lifting out a tub of sliced tomatoes from the fridge, she deliberately busied herself running over her mental accounts. It stopped her thinking about that ridiculous bouquet—and the infuriating man who'd sent it to her.

OK, so where was she in her savings? She ran the figures through her head, feeling a familiar sense of satisfaction and reassurance as she did so. She'd worked flat-out these last twelve months, and now she was almost, *almost* at the point of setting off on her dream.

To travel. To leave the UK and see the world! To make a reality of all the places she'd only ever read about. Europe, the Med, even the USA—and maybe even further...South America, the Far East and Australia.

She'd never been abroad in her life.

A sigh escaped her. She shouldn't feel deprived because she hadn't travelled abroad. Gramps hadn't liked 'abroad.' He hadn't liked foreign travel. The south coast had been about as far as he'd been prepared to go.

'Nothing wrong with Bognor,' he'd used to tell her. 'Or Brighton. Or Bournemouth.'

So that was where they'd gone for their annual summer holiday every year until she was a teenager. And for many years it had been fine—she'd loved the beach, even on her own with no brothers or sisters to play with. She'd had her grandfather, who'd raised her ever since his daughter and son-in-law had been killed in the same motorway pile-up that had killed his wife.

Looking back with adult eyes, she knew that having his five-year-old granddaughter to care for after the wholesale slaughter of the rest of his family had been her grandfather's salvation. And he, in return, had become her rock—the centre of her world, the only person in the entire universe who loved her.

When she'd finished with school and started a Business Studies degree course at a nearby college, she'd opted to continue to live at home, in the familiar semi-detached house in the north London suburb she'd grown up in.

'I'd be daft to move out, Gramps. Student accommodation costs a fortune, and most of the flats are complete dumps.'

Though she'd meant it, she'd also known that her grandfather had been relieved that she'd stayed at home with him.

It hadn't cramped her social life to be living at home still, and she'd revelled in student life like any eighteen-year-old, enjoying her fair share of dating. It hadn't been until she'd met Jak in her second year that things had become serious. He'd taken her seriously, too, seeing past her dazzling looks to the person within, and soon they'd become an item.

Had she been in love with him? She'd discovered the answer to that at the end of their studies. Not enough to dedicate her life to him the way he'd wanted her to.

'I've got a job with the charity I applied for—out in Africa. I'm going to be teaching English, building schools, digging wells. It's what I've always dreamed of.' He'd paused, looking at Mel straight on. 'Will you come with me? Support me in my work? Make your life with me?'

It had been the question she'd known was coming— the question she'd only been able to answer one way. Whether or not she'd wanted to join Jak in his life's work, it had been impossible anyway.

'I can't,' she'd said. 'I can't leave Gramps.'

Because by then that was what it had come down to. In the three years of her being a student her grandfather had aged—had crossed that invisible but irreversible boundary from being the person who had raised her and looked after her to being someone who now looked to her to look after *him*. The years had brought heart problems—angina and mini-strokes—but far worse than his growing physical frailty had been the mental frailty that had come with it. Mel had known with sadness and a sinking heart that he had become more and more dependent on her.

She hadn't been able to leave him. How could she have deserted him, the grandfather she loved so much? How could she have abandoned him when he'd needed her? She had only been able to wait, putting her own life on hold and devoting herself to the one relative she'd possessed: the grandfather who loved her.

The months had turned into years—three whole years—until finally he'd left her in the only way that a frail, ill old man could leave his granddaughter.

She'd wept—but not only from grief. There had been relief, too—she knew that. Relief for him, that at last he was freed from his failing body, his faltering mind. And relief, too, for herself.

She hadn't been able to deny, though it had hurt to think it, that now, after his death, she was freed of all responsibility. Her grandfather had escaped the travails of life and by doing so had given Mel her own life back— given back to her what she wanted most of all to claim.

Her freedom.

Freedom to do what she had long dreamt of doing. To travel! To travel as she'd never had the opportunity to do—to travel wherever the wind blew her, wherever took her fancy. See the world.

But to do that she needed money. Money she'd been unable to earn for herself when she'd become her grandfather's carer. Yes, she had some money, because her grandfather had left her his savings—but that would be needed, as a safe nest egg, for when she finally returned to the UK to settle down and build a career for herself. So to fund her longed-for travels she was working all the hours she could—Sarrie's Sarnies by day, and waitressing in a nearby restaurant by night.

And soon—oh, *very* soon—she'd be off and away. Picking up a cheap last-minute flight and heading wherever the spirit took her until the money ran out, when she'd come back home to settle down.

If she ever did come back…

Maybe I'll never come back. Maybe I'll stay foot-loose all my life. Never be tied down again by anything or anyone! Free as a bird!

Devoted as she had been to her grandfather, after years of caring for him such freedom was a heady prospect.

So, too, was the looking forward to another element of youth that she had set aside till now.

Romance.

Since Jak had gone to Africa and she'd stayed behind to look after her grandfather romance had been impossible. In the early days she'd managed to go on a couple of dates, but as her grandfather's health had worsened those moments had become less and less. But now... Oh, now romance could blossom again—and she'd welcome it with open arms.

She knew exactly what she wanted at this juncture of her life. Nothing intense or serious, as her relationship with Jak had been. Nothing long-term, as he had hoped things would be between them. No, for now all she craved was the heady buzz of eyes meeting across a crowded room, mutual desire acknowledged and fulfilled—frothy, carefree, self-indulgent fun. *That* was what she longed for now.

Her mouth curved in a cynical smile and her eyes sparked. Well, that attitude should make her popular. Men were habitually wary of women who wanted more from them—they were the ones who didn't like clingy women, who didn't want to be tied down. Who liked to enjoy their pick of women as and when they fancied.

The cynical smile deepened. She'd bet money that Nikos Parakis was a man like that. Looking her over the way he had...

As she started to serve a new customer who'd just walked in she shook her head clear of the memory. She had better things to do than speculate about the love life of Nikos Parakis—or speculate about anything to do with him at all.

Soon his extravagantly OTT flowers would fade, and so would her memory of the intemperate encounter between them today. And eventually so would the disturbingly vivid memory of the physical impact he'd made on her, with his dark, devastating looks. And that, she said to herself firmly, would be that.

'What kind of sandwich would you like?' she asked brightly of her customer, and got on with her job.

'Pull over just there,' Nikos instructed his driver, who duly slid the sleek top-of-the-range BMW to the side of the road to let his employer get out.

Emerging, Nikos glanced along the pavement, observing for a moment or two the comings and goings at the sandwich bar and wondering whether he was being a complete idiot for doing what he was about to do.

He'd reflected on the decision on the way here from the Parakis offices, changing his mind several times. The idea that had struck him the day before when faced with the prospect of enduring an evening of Fiona Pellingham trying to corner him had stayed with him, and he'd reviewed it from all angles several times. But he'd found that whenever he'd lined up all his objections—she was a complete stranger, she was bolshie, she might not even possess an evening gown suitable for the highly upmarket Viscari St James—they'd promptly all collapsed under the one overwhelming reason he *wanted* her to accompany him on Friday evening.

Which was the fact that he could not get her out of his head.

And he could think of nothing else except wanting to see her again.

The same overwhelming urge possessed him again
now—to feast his eyes on her, drink her in and feel, yet
again, that incredible visceral kick he'd got from her.
Anticipation rose pleasurably through him.

He glanced at his watch. It was near the end of the
working day so she should be shutting up shop soon—
these old-fashioned sandwich bars did not stay open in
the evening. He strolled towards the entrance, pushed
the door open with the flat of his palm and walked in.
There was only one other customer inside, and Nikos
could see he was handing over his money, taking his
wrapped sandwich with him.

Serving him was the blonde, bolshie, bad-attitude
total stunner.

Instantly Nikos's eyes went straight to her and stayed
there, riveted.

Yes! The affirmation of all that he'd remembered
about the impact she'd had on him surged through
Nikos. She was as fantastic now as she had been then.
Face, figure—the whole package. Burning right into
his retinas, all over again.

Oh, yes, definitely—most definitely—this was the right
decision to have made.

'Here's your change,' he heard her say to her customer as he paused just inside the door. Her voice was
cheerful, her expression smiling.

No sign, Nikos noted with caustic observation, of
the bolshiness she'd targeted *him* with. But what he was
noticing more was the way that her quick smile only
enhanced the perfection of her features, lending her
mouth a sinuous curve and warming her sapphire eyes.
He could feel his pulse give a discernible kick at the
sight of her smile, even though it wasn't directed at him.

What will it feel like when she smiles at me? he wondered to himself. But he knew the answer already.

Good—that was what it would feel like.

And more than good. *Inviting...*

But just as this pleasurable thought was shaping in his brain he saw her eyes glance towards the latest person to come in—himself—and immediately her expression changed. She waited only before her customer had quit the shop before launching her attack.

'What are *you* doing here?' she demanded.

Nikos strolled forward, and it gave him particular satisfaction to see her take a half-step back, defensively. It meant she felt the need to raise her defences about him—and *that* meant, he knew with every masculine instinct, that she was vulnerable to him—vulnerable to the effect he was having on her. The effect he *wanted* to have on her.

He had seen it in her eyes, in the way they had suddenly been veiled—but not soon enough to conceal the betraying leap of emotion within.

It was an emotion that was as old as time, and one he'd seen before when he'd deliberately let his gaze wash over her, making his own reaction to her beauty as tangible as a caress...

And, veiled though it had been, it told him all he needed to know. That in spite of her outward bristling towards him, behind that layer of defence, she was reacting to him as strongly, as powerfully, as he was to her.

And once again he felt satisfaction spread through him at the knowledge that she was as reactive to him as he was to her—as powerfully attracted to him as he was to her—oh, yes, most definitely.

His eyes flickered over her again. He felt an overwhelming urge to drink her in, to remind himself of just what it was she had that so drew him to her. That extraordinary beauty she possessed was undimmed, even in these workaday surroundings and even clad as she was in that unprepossessing T-shirt. She had made not the slightest adornment to her natural beauty by way of make-up or styling her hair—most of which was still concealed under that unlovely baseball cap.

'I wanted to see you again,' he told her, coming up to the counter.

She stood her ground—he could see her doing it—but her figure had stiffened.

'Why?' she countered, making her expression stony.

He ignored her question. 'Did you get my flowers?' he asked. He kept his voice casual, kept his own eyes veiled now—for the time being.

'Yes.' The single-word answer was tight and...unappreciative.

An eyebrow quirked. 'They were not to your taste?'

Her chin lifted. 'I bet you don't even know what they are. I bet you just told your secretary to send them.'

His mouth indented. 'I suspect they will be lilies,' he answered. 'My PA likes lilies.'

'Well, send them to *her* next time!' was the immediate retort.

'But my PA,' he returned, entering into the spirit of their sparring, 'was not the one I needed to apologise to. And besides...' his dark eyes glinted '...*she* wasn't the one whose mood needed improving.'

It was deliberate baiting—and unwise, considering he wanted her to accept his invitation for the evening, but he couldn't resist the enjoyment of sparring with her and it got him his reward. That coruscating sapphire flash of her eyes—making her beautiful eyes even more outstanding.

'Well, they *didn't* improve my mood,' she snapped back. 'And you standing there doesn't either. So if that's all you came here to say, then consider it said.'

'It isn't,' said Nikos. His expression changed as he abandoned the sparring and became suddenly more businesslike. 'I have an invitation to put to you.'

For a moment she looked stupefied. Then, hard on the heels of that, deeply suspicious. 'What?'

'I would like,' Nikos informed her, 'to invite you to a charity gala this Friday night.'

'What?' The word came again, and an even more stupefied look.

'Allow me to elaborate,' said Nikos, and proceeded to do so.

His veiled eyes were watching for her reaction. Despite her overt hostility he could see that she was listening. Could see, too, that she was trying not to look at him. Trying to keep her eyes blank.

Trying—and failing.

She's aware of me, responsive to me—she's fighting it, but it's there all the same.

It flickered like electricity between them as he went on.

'I find,' he told her, keeping his tone bland and neutral, so as not to set her hackles rising again, 'that at short notice I am without a "plus one" for this Friday evening—a charity gala to which I am committed.' He looked at her straight on. 'Therefore I would be highly gratified if you would agree to be that "plus one" for the occasion. I'm sure you would find it enjoyable—it's at the Viscari St James Hotel, which I hope you will agree is a memorable venue.'

He paused minutely, then allowed his mouth to indent into a swift smile.

'Please say you'll come.'

Her expression was a study, and he enjoyed watching it. Stupefaction mixed with deep, deep suspicion. And even deeper scepticism.

'And of course, Mr Parakis, you have absolutely no one else you could possibly invite except a complete stranger—someone you told to her face you'd sack if she were unfortunate enough to be one of your hapless minions!' she finally shot at him, her head going back and her eyes sparking.

He was unfazed. 'Indeed,' he replied shamelessly. 'So, if you would be kind enough to take pity on my predicament and help me in my hour of need, my gratitude would know no bounds...'

A very unladylike snort escaped her. 'Yeah, right,' she managed to say derisively.

'It's quite true,' he answered limpidly. 'I *would* be extremely grateful.'

'And I'd be a complete mug to believe you,' she shot back.

Nikos's expression changed again. 'Why? What is the problem here for you?' His eyes rested on her, conveying a message older than time. 'Do you not know how extraordinarily beautiful you are? How any man would be privileged to have you at his side—?'

He saw the colour run out over her sculpted cheekbones. Saw her swallow.

'Will you not let me invite you?' he said again. There was the slightest husk in his voice. It was there without his volition.

Mixed emotions crossed her face. 'No,' she said finally—emphatically.

His eyebrows rose. 'Why not?' he asked outright.

Hers snapped together. 'Because I don't like you—that's why!'

He gave a half-laugh, discovering he was enjoying her bluntness. 'We got off to a bad start—I admit that freely. I was hungry and short-tempered, and you gave me a hard time and I resented it.'

'You spoke to me like I was beneath you,' she shot at him. 'And you looked down your nose at Joe—wouldn't give him a penny even though you're obviously rolling in it!' She cast a pointed look at him. 'Your wallet was stuffed with fifties!'

'Did you expect me to hand a fifty over to him?' he protested. 'And for your information I gave him a handful of all those pound coins you dumped on me.'

Mel's expression changed. '*What?* Oh, God, he'll have just gone off and spent it on booze.' Her eyes narrowed. 'Did you really give him money?'

'Ask him next time he comes in for a free sandwich,' said Nikos drily. 'So…' his voice changed '…are you going to take pity on me and accept my invitation?'

She was wavering—he could tell that with every male instinct. *She wants to accept, but her pride is holding her back.*

'You know,' he said temperately as her internal conflict played out in her betraying gaze, 'I really am quite safe. And very respectable, too. As is the Viscari St James Hotel and the charity gala.'

'You're a complete stranger.'

'No, I'm not. You know who I am—you addressed me by name just now,' Nikos countered.

'Only because you put your name on the card with those flowers—and *they* were an insult anyway.'

'How so?' Nikos's astonishment was open.

The sapphire flash that made her beauty even more

outstanding came again. 'You can't even see it, can you?' she returned. 'Sending me a ludicrously over-the-top bouquet and then having the gall to tell me to improve my mood—like you hadn't caused my bad mood in the first place. It was just so...so *patronising*!'

'Patronising? I don't see why.'

Mel's screwed her face up. Emotion was running like a flash flood through her. She was trying to cope with seeing him right in front of her again, just when she'd been starting to put the whole encounter of the previous day behind her, and trying urgently to suppress her reaction to seeing him again. Trying *not* to betray just what an impact he was having on her—how her eyes wanted to gaze at him, take in that sable hair, the incredible planes and contours of his face—and trying not to let herself fall head first into those dark eyes of his...

She was trying to use anger to keep him at bay—but he kept challenging it, eroding it. Throwing at her that ludicrous invitation which had stopped her dead in her tracks—an invitation which was as over-the-top as that vast bouquet had been.

'Yes,' she insisted, 'patronising. Mr Rich and Lordly sending flowers to Poor Little Shop Girl!'

There was a moment's silence. Then Nikos spoke. 'I did not mean it that way.' He took a breath. 'I told you—I sent them with the intention of making amends once I realised I had been rude to you—in more ways than one.'

He avoided spelling out what he was referring to, but he knew she was thinking about it for he could see a streak of colour heading out across her cheekbones again.

'But if you want me to apologise for sending the flowers as well, then—'

She cut across him. 'No, it's all right,' she said. She tried not to sound truculent. OK, so he hadn't meant to come across as patronising. Fine. She could be OK with that. She could be OK with him apologising to her. And she could be fine with him giving money to Joe, even if he *would* just go and spend it all on alcohol.

But what she *couldn't* be fine with was what he was asking her.

To go out with him. Go out with a man who set her pulse racing, who seemed to be able to slam right past every defence she put up against him—a man she wanted to gaze at as shamelessly, blatantly, as he had looked at her.

What's he doing to me? And how? And why am I being like this? Why can't I just tell him to go so I can shut the shop and never see him again and just get on with my life?

And why don't I want to do that?

But she knew why—and it was in every atom of Nikos Parakis, standing there across the counter, asking her why she didn't want to go out with him.

'Look, Mr Parakis, I don't know what this is about— I really don't. You set eyes on me for the second time in your life and suddenly you're asking me out for the evening? It's weird—bizarre.'

'Let me be totally upfront with you about why I'm asking *you*, in particular, to come with me on Friday evening,' he answered.

His eyes were resting on her, but not with any expression in them that made her either angry, suspicious or, worst of all, vulnerable to his overwhelming sexual allure.

'I'm in an awkward situation,' he said bluntly. 'Whilst in London I find myself committed to this charity gala tomorrow night, at the Viscari St James. Unfortunately, also present will be a woman whom I know through business and who is, alas, harbouring possessive intentions towards me which I cannot reciprocate.'

Was there an edge in his voice? Mel wondered. But he was continuing.

'I do not wish to spend the evening fending her off, let alone giving her cause to think that her hopes might be fulfilled. But I don't wish to wound or offend her either, and nor do I wish to sour any future business dealings. I need a…graceful but persuasive way to deflect her. Arriving with my own "plus one" would, I hope, achieve that. However, the lady in hot pursuit of me knows perfectly well that I am currently unattached— hence my need to discover a sufficiently convincing partner for the evening to thwart her hopes.'

His expression changed again.

'All of which accounts for my notion that inviting a fantastically beautiful complete stranger as my "plus one" would be the ideal answer to my predicament,' he finished, keeping his gaze steady on Mel's face.

He paused. His eyes rested on her with an unreadable expression that Mel could not match.

'You fit the bill perfectly,' he said. And now, suddenly, his expression was not unreadable at all…

As she felt the unveiled impact of his gaze Mel heard her breath catch, felt emotion swing into her as if it had been blown in on the wind from an opened door. He was offering her an experience she'd never had in her life—a glittering evening out with the most breathtakingly attractive man she'd ever seen.

So why not? What are you waiting for? Why hesitate for a moment?

She thought of all the reasons she shouldn't go—he

might be the most ridiculously good-looking and most ludicrously attractive man she'd ever seen, but he was also the most infuriating and arrogant and self-satisfied man she'd ever met.

But he's apologised, and his self-satisfaction comes with a sense of humour about it, and he's given me a cogent reason for his out-of-the-blue invitation...

But he was a complete stranger and could be anyone.

I know his name—and, anyway, he's talking about a posh charity bash at a swanky West End hotel, not an orgy in an opium den...

But she had nothing suitable to wear for such a thing as a posh charity bash at a swanky West End hotel.

Yes, I have—I've got that second-hand designer evening gown I bought in a charity shop that was dead cheap because it had a stain on it. I can cover the stain with a corsage...and I can make the corsage from that over-the-top bunch of lilies he's just sent...

But she ought to be working—she made good tips on a Friday night at the restaurant.

Well, I can work an extra shift on Sunday lunchtime instead, when Sarrie's is closed...

One by one she could hear herself demolishing her own objections against accepting Nikos Parakis's invitation. Heard herself urging on the one overwhelming reason for accepting it.

A little thrill went through her.

She was about to start a new life—her *own* life. She would be free of obligations to anyone else. Free to do what she wanted and go where she wanted. Free to indulge herself finally!

And when it came to indulgence what could be more self-indulgent than a gorgeous, irresistible man like the one standing in front of her? It was just too, too tempting to turn down.

If anything could herald her new life's arrival with the sound of trumpets it must surely be this. So why not grab the opportunity with both hands?

Why not?

'Well,' she heard him say, one eyebrow quirked expectantly, 'what's the verdict? Do we have a deal?'

Her eyelids dipped briefly over her eyes and she felt a smile start to form at her mouth.

'OK, then,' she said. 'Yes, we have a deal.'

CHAPTER THREE

MEL TWISTED AS best she could, but it was no good. She couldn't possibly see her full length reflection in the tiny mirror she'd got propped up on top of the filing cabinet where Sarrie kept the accounts.

Well, it didn't matter. She knew the dress suited her because she'd loved it from the moment she'd first seen it in the charity shop. It was the prize piece in the collection she'd been scouring charity shops for over the last year, putting together a cut-price but stylish wardrobe for her foreign travels.

The dress was silk, but in very fine plissé folds, which made it ideal for travelling as she could just twist it into a roll for packing. The colour suited her perfectly, she knew, because the pale blue was shot with a deeper hyacinth-blue, with a touch of lilac to it that set off her eyes. And its simple folds suited her preference for unfussy, 'no bling' styles.

With the reassurance of its designer label she knew she could go anywhere in it—even the Viscari St James. She'd looked up the hotel on Sarrie's PC and had whistled. It had a cachet that was way, way beyond any place she'd ever set foot in. But that was hardly surprising—for the internet had also revealed to her that Nikos Parakis was the scion of the Parakis banking dynasty—a

Greek-based outfit that seemed to be rolling in it to the tune of *zillions*.

And he came slumming along into a humble sandwich bar! she thought with mordant humour. No wonder he'd been so outraged at her lack of awed deference.

But, to his credit, he had at least apologised, and she'd draw a line under it. Now, she realised, she was simply looking forward to seeing him again. Would they still spar with each other?

She found a smile quirking her lips at the prospect... And, of course, at the prospect of feasting her eyes on the paean to male gorgeousness that was the very, *very* gorgeous Nikos Parakis.

Eyes glinting in anticipation of the treat that she knew this evening would be, she picked up the little satin clutch bag that went with her dress. Time to get going. Nikos had told her a car would collect her, and it was nearly the specified pickup time now.

She stepped outside on to the pavement, carefully locking up as she went and dropping the keys into her clutch, aware of a sleek, chauffeured car humming quietly and expensively at the kerb. She headed purposefully towards it, getting used to the unaccustomed feel of high heels and long skirts and her hair being loosened from its usual workaday tied-back plait.

As she approached the car the driver got out, tipping his cap to her in salutation, and from the very male expression in his eyes she knew she looked good enough for the evening ahead.

And for the man who was making it possible.

A little flutter of happy anticipation went through her as she got gracefully into the car when the door was held open for her. It had been so, so long since she'd gone out at all for the evening—and never like this, in such luxury and elegance.

The flutter came again, and she settled back happily to enjoy the chauffeured car, with its soft leather seats, its wide footwell lined with dove-grey carpet, and its fittings all in polished marquetry, as she was driven to her glamorous destination—and to the breathtakingly devastating man who awaited her there.

Her wonderful new life of freedom was just beginning, and this gorgeous, *gorgeous* man was just the person to start it off for her.

Nikos strolled up to the bar and placed his order. He did not sit down—merely propped one forearm on the gleaming mahogany surface, rested his foot on the brass rail and glanced around. The resplendent Edwardian-style bar just off the equally resplendent lobby at the Viscari St James was a popular watering hole for the well heeled. Many, like him, were in tuxedos, gathering for the evening's main function—the charity gala.

His mood, as he glanced around, was mixed. Happy anticipation filled him—his driver had phoned a while ago to inform him that he was en route, and soon—very soon—he was going to see just how even more fantastically beautiful his date for the evening looked in evening dress.

But he also felt a momentary doubt assail him. Would she possess the kind of attire that was appropriate for the Viscari? Perhaps he should have offered to help in that department? Then he quashed the thought—he was pretty sure that any such offer, however well intentioned, would have got shot down as 'patronising'. No, if having nothing to wear had been a problem she'd have said so.

He barely had time to take a first mellowing sip of his dry martini, directing another sweeping glance around the room, before he stilled.

She was walking into the bar area.

His eyes went to her immediately—it was impossible for them not to. Dimly, he was aware that he was far from being the only male whose eyes had gone straight to her. *Thee mou*, but she could turn heads!

And as for any concerns that she might not possess the kind of dress that was suited to a venue like the Viscari St James...they evaporated like a drop of water on a hot stove.

She looked stunning—*beyond* stunning.

Finally he could see just what nature had bestowed upon her, now untrammelled and unconcealed by her workaday appearance as it had been so far.

She was tall and slender, but with curves that went in and out in all the right places that were perfectly enhanced by the elegant fall of the ankle-length gown she was wearing. Its style and colour were perfect for her—a blending of delicate shades of blue and lilac. Her shoulders were swathed in soft folds of the multi-hued material, and the décolletage was draped but not low-cut. A creamy white corsage nestled in the drapery, and Nikos's mouth gave a quirk of amusement. He was pretty sure the corsage originated from the bouquet of lilies he'd had sent to her.

As for her hair—finally he could see what he'd wanted to see of it, freed from that obnoxious baseball cap. It was everything he could have wanted, loosened and swept back from her face, caught to one side with a mother of pearl comb before curving around one shoulder in a long, lush golden fall.

And her face— *Ah*... Nikos thought, satisfaction running through him with an even greater intensity. He had thought her stunningly beautiful when she'd had not a scrap of make-up on, but now, with her luminous eyes deepened, their lashes lengthened, her cheekbones delineated and her mouth, like a ripe damson...

He stepped forward, his smile deepening.

She saw him immediately—he could tell. Could tell, too, that the impact he was making on her was everything he'd wanted. His sense of satisfaction intensified again.

Her eyes widened with telltale revelation as she made her way towards him. And as she came up to him for the first time Nikos could detect a dent in her air of self-assured composure. Two spots of colour burned briefly but revealingly in her sculpted cheeks.

His eyes were warm upon her. 'You look fantastic,' he breathed.

His compliment drew a new expression from her face.

'I rather thought that was the idea,' Mel said.

Her voice was dry. But she needed it to be. She needed it to be because as her eyes had alighted upon Nikos Parakis she had felt a kick go through her that she had not intended to feel. If he'd looked drop-dead gorgeous before, in his handmade suit, now, in a handmade tux, he looked ten times more deadly.

And as for the sensation going through her now, as his dark gold-flecked eyes worked over her... She could feel awareness shooting through her, sky-high. Urgently she sought to quell it, to stay composed and unruffled.

Nikos's smile deepened. 'What can I get you to drink?' he asked.

'Sparkling mineral water is fine, thank you,' she managed to get out, without sounding too breathless.

He glanced at her. 'Do you not drink alcohol?'

'Oh, yes,' she replied, more easily now, glad to find her voice sounding a little more normal. 'But I assume there will be wine with dinner, so I don't want to make a start on it yet.'

'Very wise,' Nikos murmured, and relayed her order to the barman.

Then he turned his attention back to his date for the evening. A date, he suddenly realised with a sense of confusion, whose name he had absolutely no idea of!

Up to now, in his head, she'd simply been the stunning blonde in the sandwich shop. He blinked for a moment. Then, to his relief, he realised that of *course* he knew her name. It had been emblazoned on that unlovely T-shirt she'd been wearing in the sandwich bar.

The barman placed a glass of iced sparking water on the counter. Nikos picked it up and handed it to her. 'There you go, Sarrie,' he said, with a smile.

She took it, but stared at him. 'Sarrie…?' she echoed.

Nikos frowned slightly. 'You prefer not to be called that?' he checked.

She gave him a look. 'Well, no, actually—because it's not my name. *Sarrie*,' she elucidated, giving him another look—one that reminded him of their first sparking encounter, 'is the name of the guy who owns the sandwich bar—hence "Sarrie's Sarnies." *My* name,' she informed him, 'is Mel.'

She paused minutely.

'Do you require a surname? Or is that a complete irrelevance because after all,' she said lightly, 'our acquaintance is going to be terminated after tonight?'

Nikos found himself frowning. *Was* their acquaintance gong to be terminated after tonight? Was that what he intended?

Do I want this to be the only time I spend with her?

Did he really want this incredible, fantastic-looking, stunningly gorgeous blonde who was making his senses reel to be with him only for one single evening?

As his eyes flickered over her he knew what his body wanted him to answer—oh, yes, indeed! No doubt about that in the slightest. But it wasn't just his body responding to the overwhelming physical attraction he felt for this fantastically beautiful woman.

What was she like as a person? As an individual? Oh, he knew she could stand up to him—stand her ground and spark verbal fire with him—but how much more was there to her than that?

Time to find out...

He smiled a warm, encompassing smile. 'Mel,' he asked her, 'don't you realise yet that I want to know a lot more about you than just your surname?'

To his distinct satisfaction he saw once again that telltale colour run fleetingly over her sculpted cheekbones. He let his gaze have the effect he wanted, and then deliberately let it soften as he relaxed against the burnished mahogany surface of the bar.

Her colour was still heightened when she answered him. 'Well, it's Cooper—just in case you should need to know. Like when you introduce me to this woman you want me to keep at bay for you.'

There was an acerbic tinge to her voice, but Nikos ignored it.

I would want her here tonight even if Fiona Pellingham were a hundred miles away.

The knowledge was sure in his head—the certainty of it absolute. Mel Cooper—so fiery and so fantastically beautiful—was a woman he wanted to know more about. *Much* more.

'So, tell me, Mel Cooper,' he said, 'first of all how do you come to be working in an establishment rejoicing in the name of "Sarrie's Sarnies"?'

Deliberately he kept his tone light, with mild humour in it. He could see her recovering her composure. The slight stain of colour ebbed. She took a sip of water from her glass. Her voice, when she spoke, had lost its acerbic tone and he was glad.

'Sarrie Silva is the uncle of a friend of mine, and he offered me the job,' she explained. 'The pay isn't bad, and I actually enjoy the work.' No need to tell him that in comparison with looking after her grandfather day in and day out for years *any* kind of alternative work was bliss. 'And best of all he lets me use the back room as a bedroom, so I effectively live there.'

Nikos's eyebrows rose. 'You *live* in the back room of a sandwich bar?'

'Yes, it's rent-free—and in London that counts for a hell of a lot,' Mel answered feelingly.

'How long have you been living like that?' Nikos asked.

'Nearly a year now. Ever since I had to move out of my childhood home.'

Nikos frowned. 'Why did you have to do that?'

'It was after my grandfather died. I'd...looked after him...' She could hear her voice twist, feel her throat tighten, feel the familiar grief at his loss ache within her, and hurried on. 'When I lost him...' the twist in her voice was more pronounced, though she tried to cover it '...I decided I'd rather rent out the house, because that would give me some steady income.'

'But you became homeless?' Nikos objected.

She gave a quick shake of her head, smiling now. 'That

didn't matter, because it was only ever going to be temporary. I'll be off abroad soon,' she explained.

She said it deliberately. It had occurred to her as she spoke that it would be prudent to make it clear to Nikos Parakis that she was going to be out of London very soon. His words to her after she'd made that jibe at him just now echoed in her head.

'Don't you realise yet that I want to know a lot more about you than just your surname?'

Echoed dangerously…

Dangerously because all she wanted to do was enjoy this evening, enjoy the lavish luxury of her surroundings and keep as tight a lid as possible on the totally predictable effect Nikos Parakis was having on her female sensibilities.

Definitely time to make it clear that she was not hanging about in London for long. This evening was nothing more than an unexpected and most important a one-off treat—one she would enjoy, make the most of, and then consign to memory. And Nikos Parakis with it.

His dark eyebrows had come together when she'd mentioned going abroad.

'Where are you thinking of travelling to?' he asked.

'No idea,' she replied insouciantly, taking a sip of her water. 'Spain, probably—wherever I can get a cheap flight to.'

He looked slightly startled. 'You have no destination in mind?'

'Not really. I just want to travel—that's all. So any place is as good as another.' Her voice changed. 'Wherever I go it will be an adventure.'

Nikos took another sip of his martini. 'Where have you travelled so far in your life?' he asked.

'Nowhere. That's the whole point,' Mel replied.

There was emotion in her voice—Nikos could hear it. He could also see the enthusiasm in her face…the excitement. Could see, too, how it made her eyes sparkle, lighting up her face. Enhancing her stunning beauty.

It was a beauty, he knew, from all his long-honed masculine experience, that would cause total havoc amongst the entire male population of the world once she was out in it. Probably too much havoc…

'Are you going with friends?' he asked.

Behind his innocuous question he knew another one lurked. *Are you going with a boyfriend...?*

But of course she wasn't. If she were, she wouldn't have accepted his invitation tonight, would she?

The knowledge that she was unattached gave him satisfaction. More satisfaction than her answer to his question.

Mel shook her head. 'No, just solo. I'm sure I'll make friends as I go.'

'Well, be careful,' he found himself warning her. 'There are parts of the world where solo travellers—let alone female ones—are not advised to go.'

Her mouth tightened. 'I can look after myself.'

Nikos's expression was wry. 'Yes, I know,' he said, his voice dry. 'You can go twelve rounds verbally—no problem. But…' He held up a hand. 'All the same, stick to tourist areas—that's my advice.'

For a moment it looked as if she was going to argue the point, for he could see the warlike sparkle in her eyes. Then it subsided.

'OK, OK…' Mel temporised. 'I'll hire a bodyguard and lug him around with me—I get the picture,' she said, in a deliberately resigned voice.

'An excellent idea,' Nikos murmured, humour in his eyes. 'I can recommend a first-class firm offering the kind of close personal protection which I have, on occasion, engaged myself.'

Mel's expression changed. 'Good grief—are you serious?'

Nikos nodded. 'There are some…let us say *restless* places in the world, where it is advisable to have someone riding shotgun beside you.'

Her eyes widened. 'Why do you go to such places?'

'I do business there,' he answered drily. Then, at the questioning and indeed wary look in her eyes, he went on swiftly. 'And, no, before your fervid imagination carries you away, I am *not* an arms dealer. I am a very boring and tediously respectable banker,' he informed her.

'Yes, I know,' she admitted. 'I looked you up. Just in case,' she said dulcetly. 'Though of course,' she went on, allowing herself a provocative glance at him, 'I didn't think bankers *were* very respectable these days…' She paused, quirking an eyebrow questioningly. 'Or should that be *respected*?'

'Ouch!' said Nikos. He took another mouthful of his martini. 'Given the sorry economic state of the world, and the role that reckless lending by the banks has played in that, I can appreciate your scepticism. *However*,' he stressed, 'what banks *should* be doing—what I strive to do myself—is *aid* business recovery. Primarily for the Parakis Bank in Greece, which has been so badly hit by recession, but also in other parts of the world, as well.'

She was looking at him with an interested expression—no dumb blonde, it seemed—and the knowledge gladdened him.

He went on with his explication. 'The Parakis Bank is an investment bank, and we have always strived for genuine partnership with our clients—which means we take a financial hit if they lose money. It also means we have to choose clients very carefully—reckless, over-ambitious companies run by greedy, lazy people who want only to enrich themselves are not on our books. I look for clients who have a passion for the sector they are in, who understand the global trends in their markets and know where opportunities lie—who have worked hard to build their businesses so far, and who simply need a loan to get them to the next level, which is what we provide, to our mutual benefit.'

He smiled at her.

'So, have I convinced you that not all bankers are evil incarnate?' His voice was infused with wry humour.

Mel looked at him. 'It *sounds* persuasive,' she conceded.

'And are you persuadable?' he pressed.

His stance had changed subtly, and so had his tone. She heard it and broke eye contact, making herself glance away briefly, then looking back again. There was a subtext going on, she knew. One that had nothing to do with the banking industry.

She flashed a smile at him. Deliberately coruscating. Deliberately calling him on his challenge.

'Sometimes,' she said.

She let the ambiguity hang in the air. He wanted subtext—she could do subtext. Or so he could think if he wanted. Which it seemed he did. She saw long eyelashes dip over his dark expressive eyes.

'How very reassuring,' he murmured, and again Mel knew the subject was not banking or finance.

She made a face, abandoning her pose of ambiguity.

'Well, you knew that anyway, didn't you? I mean, you persuaded me to turn up here tonight,' she exclaimed, in a half-exasperated tone.

'And how incredibly glad I am that I did,' he answered, his voice openly warm. 'Or I would have missed out on having the most beautiful woman in London on my arm and being the envy of every male here.'

There was humour in his voice, too, and Mel gave a laughing shake of her head at the over-the-top compliment.

'Yeah, yeah...' she said with good humour, playing down his over-the-top compliment. Even as she spoke, though, she could feel a little thrill of gratification go through her that he had given it.

She drained the last of her mineral water and replaced the glass on the bar. 'So...' she changed the subject '...do we actually get to eat tonight? It might sound weird, considering I work in a sandwich shop, but I never get time for lunch and I'm totally starving.'

'Excellent,' said Nikos. 'The food here is outstanding—even when you're dining *en masse* as we shall be doing—so a hearty appetite is a distinct advantage.' He threw an assessing glance at her slender figure. 'I do hope you're not the type of woman who considers two lettuce leaves a feast?'

Mel laughed again. 'Not tonight, I promise you,' she assured him.

'Excellent,' he said again. 'In which case, shall we go through? I see people are beginning to make a move.'

He set his own empty martini glass on the bar and with the slightest flourish proffered his arm to Mel with a very small bow.

'Sounds good,' she said, and hooked her hand over his sleeve. 'Lead me to the food!'

Long lashes swept over dark, dark eyes, not quite hiding the glint within. 'I am yours to command,' Nikos murmured, and started to escort her forward.

Mel cocked her head at him. 'You might live to regret that rash offer,' she riposted, a smile audible in her voice.

Deep within the dark eyes that glint came again. 'I regret nothing about you whatsoever, Mel, I do assure you,' was his murmured answer.

She gave a low laugh and felt in excellent humour, for tonight was turning out to be even more enjoyable than she'd hoped it would be—and it wasn't because of the fancy venue and the chance to dress up to the nines, much as she appreciated both of those factors.

No, it was the man at her side who was giving her that buzz—as if she'd already drunk a glass of champagne and it was fizzing in her veins. The man whose strong arm was beneath her lightly resting hand, whose tall figure was at her side, and whose long-lashed, dark glinting glance was making her heart beat that enticingly bit faster...

Careful! a voice in her head was whispering, low, but urgent. *You're only with him for a single evening—remember that! So enjoy the next few hours, enjoy Nikos Parakis—his gorgeous looks, the sparky fun you're having with him—then walk away and put it in the memory box.*

She heard the voice—listened to it and knew it was telling her the truth. But as she walked out of the bar on Nikos Parakis's arm she could still feel her heart beating just that bit faster than it had ever done before...

CHAPTER FOUR

'OH, MY WORD!' Mel's exclamation was instantaneous and audible.

'Impressive, isn't it?' murmured Nikos.

'And then some.'

Mel was gazing around her at the ballroom of the hotel, now filling up with other guests taking their places for the evening. The room was quite a sight, its opulent *fin de siècle* Edwardian decor of gilding and gold satin drapery enhanced tonight by an array of damask-covered tables, each adorned with its own candelabrum and floral arrangement, as well as the glitter of crystal and silver.

Nikos led her forward. It felt good to have her on his arm. Good for multiple reasons. The main one, he reminded himself, was that having a fantastic-looking female on his arm was exactly what he'd planned for this evening to keep Fiona Pellingham at bay. But he was also increasingly aware, with every minute he was spending in Mel's company, that even without the other woman's presence here tonight, he would still want Mel with him.

Thee mou, what man wouldn't want this golden-haired goddess at his side? What man wouldn't desire her…?

'I think that's our table—just over there,' he murmured, pulling his thoughts to heel, indicating their places with a slight nod.

As they approached he realised that one of the several guests already seated was the woman whose presence had inspired him to make his choice of partner for this evening. Fiona Pellingham had turned her dark brunette head towards him and was levelling her dusky gaze at him with an intensity that made him even more glad of Mel at his side.

'That's her, isn't it?' he heard Mel say out of the corner of her mouth in a low voice. 'The pesky female who's got the unrequited hots for you?'

'Alas, yes,' Nikos replied. 'And it would seem,' he went on, his voice low, too, 'that she has taken exception to your presence.'

Fiona's gaze was, indeed, gimlet-eyed, and Nikos could see that his arrival with Mel on his arm was *not* what the other woman had wanted to see.

'What a pity,' Mel returned.

There was a sweet acidity in her voice now, and Nikos glanced at her.

'Don't let her put you down.' he said, with sudden warning in his voice.

A shaft of concern went through him. Fiona Pellingham was a high-flying career professional in a top job—and she hadn't got there by being sweetness and light to others…especially to other women.

But his concern was unnecessary.

'I wouldn't dream of it,' Mel assured him sweetly, and Nikos was instantly reminded of just how unputdownable Mel could be. He should know!

As they joined their table the other men present got to their feet and Nikos greeted them. He knew one or two professionally, and Fiona introduced the others. His greeting to Fiona was urbane—and hers, he noted observantly, was unruffled: a manner that did not go with the assessing expression in her eyes when they turned to the fabulous blonde beauty on Nikos's arm as he introduced his dinner partner.

'Hi,' said Mel casually, with a dazzling smile.

With not the slightest sign of apprehension she settled herself down at the table in one of the two remaining spaces. Nikos took his place beside her, opposite Fiona. He could see that the other males present were taking in Mel's fantastic looks, despite the presence of their own partners.

A waiter glided up to the table and started the business of pouring wine and water, while another circled with bread rolls.

Mel shook out the stiff linen napkin at her place and draped it over her lap. Then she dug into the basket of warm bread rolls and helped herself.

'I skipped lunch,' she said cheerfully, and reached for the butter dish, where tiny pats of butter floated in iced water.

She busied herself tearing the bread roll in half and applying butter to it while all around her the rest of the party started to chat. The conversation was mostly about how they knew or knew of each other, and that, Mel realised, was through their work—which was, not surprisingly, all to do with finance, corporate stuff and the City in general.

She tucked into her roll and with half an ear listened to the chit-chat. With the other half she took the measure of the female whose intentions towards Nikos Parakis she was here to block.

Fiona Pellingham was very, very attractive, with her svelte, chic brunette looks enhanced by a clearly top-end designer evening dress in deep ruby-red. Mel had quickly assessed that Fiona was very much put out about her own presence.

The other two women present were not in Fiona's league looks-wise, but they were dressed elegantly for the evening and had the appearance of being long-time partners of the men they were with.

Everyone, Mel decided, seemed perfectly amiable members of their own class and background—which was about a thousand times more privileged than her own. But so what? She wasn't picking up hostility from anyone except Fiona, and she was being accepted for what she was: namely, Nikos Parakis's 'plus one' for the evening.

While the others chatted away in their well-bred tones, talking about the City, business and the financial world in general—which Mel found out of her league, but interesting for that very reason—she settled down to make the most of what was clearly going to be a gourmet meal.

A delicious-looking salmon terrine proved as smooth and light as she could want. It was washed down very nicely, she discovered, with the crisp, cold Chablis that was served with it.

She was just setting down her glass, enjoying the delicate bouquet, when she realised she was being directly addressed.

'So, what line are *you* in, Mel?'

It was the man sitting next to Fiona who had addressed her. The question had been politely asked, and Mel saw no reason not to answer in the same way. At her side, though, she could sense that Nikos had gone on the alert, ready to intervene. But she ignored him.

'FMCG,' she replied easily. 'Food retail. I've been

researching market segmentation and seasonal versus time-of-day product-matching against predicted demand.'

'Interesting,' her questioner responded. 'Are you with one of the big retail analysts?'

Mel shook her head. 'No, this is independent research—directly customer-facing.'

Beside her, she could swear she heard Nikos make a noise in his throat that sounded distinctly like a choke.

'What will you be doing with the data?' This from one of the others around the table.

'Oh, it will go to my client to support his expansion strategy,' she answered airily.

'And is that something that the Parakis Bank will be funding?'

Fiona's voice was superficially sweet, but Mel could hear the needles in it.

Before she could reply, though, Nikos's voice interceded. 'I'd have to wait until turnover reaches an appropriate level,' Mel heard him say. His voice was dry.

She turned to him, her eyes glinting. 'I'll hold you to that,' she said lightly.

Then, deciding that Sarrie's business expansion plans—let alone her own role in his business—had better not get any more probing right now from all these high-powered City folk who dealt in turnovers of millions of pounds, she changed the subject. Time to disarm Fiona...

'Nikos was telling me,' she said, directly addressing the other woman, 'what a rising star you are, and how much you've achieved.' She made her voice warm and her smile genuine.

A slightly startled, but gratified expression crossed

Fiona's face. 'Well, it's been hard work,' she acknowledged.

There was a definite thaw in her voice now—Mel was sure of it. She pressed on.

'How real is the glass ceiling in the City?' she asked, and widened her question to include the other two women there. 'You seem to be unhindered by it.' She went back to Fiona and let her approbation show in her face.

'It does take determination to break through it,' Fiona replied.

One of the other women nodded in agreement. 'And not having babies,' she exclaimed feelingly.

'The dreaded "mommy track".' Mel grimaced. 'It's still the ultimate dilemma, isn't it, for women? Career versus family.'

Just as she'd hoped, the conversation took off along the well-trodden path of whether high-flying women could have babies without jeopardising their careers and she left them to it. It was a vigorous debate, with one of the female guests strongly defensive about the 'mommy track', and Fiona and the other woman saying bluntly that families would just have to wait.

At Mel's side, she felt Nikos lean closer in to her.

'FMCG?' she heard him query heavily. One arched eyebrow was lifted interrogatively.

Mel turned to him and smiled sweetly. 'Fast-moving consumer goods—surely you know *that*, Nikos?'

His dark eyes glinted. 'And so do you, it seems.' His voice was dry now, with a hint of surprise in it.

Mel's gaze was limpid. 'Yes, the knowledge came courtesy of my degree in Business Studies,' she murmured. 'Oh, don't tell me you thought I was just a little blonde bimbo, Nikos, sweetie?' she mused.

The glint which was so becoming familiar to her showed in his eyes. 'Only if I feel like living dangerously,' he replied, the resigned humour in his voice audible.

Mel shot him a flashing smile of approval. 'Smart guy,' she said, with a quirk of her mouth.

'You know, I'm beginning to think I *am*. Inviting you tonight was the smartest thing I've done in quite a while,' Nikos replied, and there was something in his voice that told Mel he wasn't talking about her brainpower any more.

A tiny ripple of heat went down her veins.

Careful! The voice inside her head was sharp, and instant.

She was grateful to hear herself addressed by someone else. The question came from Fiona.

'And where do you stand yourself on the "mommy track"?'

Mel answered without hesitation. 'I'm afraid I'm pretty much indelibly focussed on personal goals and priorities at the moment,' she said, not elaborating to say that travel and globetrotting were those personal goals and priorities—not building a glittering career in FMCG data analysis. 'So right now,' she added feelingly, 'I'd definitely say I don't want a baby. Of course,' she allowed, 'I'm nowhere near your level, and never likely to be, so the whole "mommy track" thing wouldn't be the issue for me as it is for you.'

Again, her compliment on Fiona's high-powered career was well-received by its target. Mel could almost see her preening.

'Mind you,' she went on, 'there is another tricky issue that female high-flyers hit, which is the shortage of suitable partners for you in the first place. It's a pretty brutal truth that men "date down"—I mean, look at *me*. Here I am, a humble retail analyst, and I get to hang out with a guy whose family own a *bank*!'

'So how *did* you?' The needles were back in Fiona's voice.

Mel smiled disarmingly. 'Oh, Nikos can be so very… *persuasive* when he sets his mind to it,' she purred, in an outrageously over-the-top style, clearly meant to be humorous, that drew a laugh from the other guests.

Even Fiona smiled, and Mel was glad. She didn't blame the other woman for setting her sights on Nikos Parakis. She wouldn't have blamed *any* woman for doing so. With or without a bank in his family, Nikos was the kind of man that every female in town would make a beeline for.

And go weak at the knees over.

Like I'm doing?

The darting question—warning?—came before she could stop it.

At her side she could hear his deep tones take up the conversational baton.

'You've no idea how hard I had to work to get Mel here,' Nikos was saying lightly. 'In the end I think it was this venue that swung it for her.'

'It's certainly fabulous,' she agreed warmly, glancing around once more at the opulent ballroom.

'All the Viscari hotels have this level of cachet,' one of men commented. 'Something that sets them apart from the common run of luxury hotels.'

'Oh, yes, absolutely,' enthused his partner. 'I think my favourite so far has to be the one in Florence.'

The conversation moved into a lively discussion about just which of the ultra-luxurious Viscari hotels was the very best of all, and Mel left them to it.

The main course was being served, and she got stuck in with definite enthusiasm. The lamb melted in her mouth, and the Burgundy washed it down to perfection.

'To think I was going to turn this down,' she murmured sideways to Nikos.

He turned his head to glance down at her. 'Enjoying yourself?'

'Oh, yes,' she breathed. 'You know, I could definitely, *definitely* get used to this.'

Something flickered across his eyes. 'Well, enjoy...' he murmured, and reached for his wine glass.

Mel found she was lifting hers, too. There was a clink as the rims met together.

'To all my good ideas, Mel,' he murmured, and his eyes were like dark, melting chocolate.

Except that the melting sensation seemed to be inside her as he spoke.

She took a mouthful of the wine, hoping it would steady her, then got back to focussing on the gourmet food she was eating. That, at least, was a safe thing to do.

Beside her, Nikos's long lashed eyes rested on her averted face. There was speculation in his gaze. As if he were asking himself a question.

A question that had the dazzling beauty that was Mel Cooper at its heart.

Mel sighed luxuriously and leant her head back against the soft leather headrest of the car seat. 'This,' she announced extravagantly, 'has been the best evening *ever.*'

Nikos, sitting beside her in the back of the chauffeur-driven car, turned his head towards her and smiled. 'I'm glad you enjoyed yourself,' he replied.

'Definitely,' she assured him, turning towards him.

Their eyes met. Mel could see, even in the dim light of the car's interior as it made its way through the nearly deserted streets of London long after the midnight hour, that there was an expression in them that made half of her want to pull her own gaze away immediately, because that was the most prudent thing to do, and half of her want to go on letting her gaze entwine with his.

For a moment she almost let her gaze slide away—then didn't. The evening was going to end very soon now, and she was going to make the most of the short time left.

Make the most of Nikos.

He was just too damn gorgeous for her to do anything else.

It was a thought that had been forming all evening and now, with the end fast approaching, cocooned in the privacy of the car, she let herself indulge in the last luxury of gazing at him, drinking him in. She could feel the wine she had drunk with dinner filling her veins, could feel its effects upon her, but she didn't care. Right now it seemed good—*very* good—just to enjoy the moment.

'That's a pretty definite vote of approval,' Nikos said. His mouth quirked.

She tilted her head slightly. She must remind herself of just why Nikos had taken her with him this evening. Not for her own sake, but to serve as a foil against another woman's unwanted attentions. It would be sensible not to forget that. Especially when they were alone together in this confined space, with the driver behind his screen and the anonymous streets beyond.

'Do you think Fiona will try and pursue you again?' she asked.

The quirk deepened. 'Hopefully not.' The dark eyes were veiled as his long lashes swept down momentarily. 'Not now you've introduced her to Sven.'

Mel gave a gurgle of laughter. 'He's not called *Sven*,' she remonstrated. 'He's called Magnus—and anyway his name doesn't matter. Only that he's a Viking hunk and runs some trendy Nordic telecoms company, which means that Fiona can consider him dateable.'

'Let's hope he considers *her* dateable. It was *you* he was chatting up when you disappeared off to the powder room,' Nikos retorted.

There was, he realised as he spoke, a discernible bite in his voice. Seeing Mel walk back to their table with the 'Viking hunk' at her side had sent a primitive growl through him. Only when she'd made a point of introducing the Viking to Fiona and leaving them to it had the growl subsided.

'I let him—precisely because I wanted to hand him over to Fiona,' Mel riposted. 'I felt genuinely bad, cutting her out—she needed a consolation prize.'

'Well, I hope Sven keeps her busy—and away from *me*,' he replied.

'Happy to have been of use.' Mel smiled with exaggerated sweetness.

'And I'm *very* grateful to you, I assure you...'

There was a husk in Nikos's voice as he spoke—she could hear it. Could feel it vibrating deep within her. The humour of a moment ago was gone, and suddenly the breath was tight in Mel's lungs.

She knew she had to break that gaze holding her motionless like this, making her breathless, but it was impossible to move. Impossible to breathe. Impossible to do anything other than just sit there, her head turned towards Nikos, feeling him so close, so very, *very* close to her...

Then she realised something had changed. The car

had stopped moving. She jerked forward, jolting her gaze free to look out of the passenger seat window.

'We're here,' she said. Her voice sounded staccato.

Breaking that compelling, unbreakable gaze had freed her. Freed her to get out of the car, go back into Sarrie's sandwich bar and bid farewell to the evening. Farewell to Nikos Parakis.

A terrible sense of flatness assailed her. The evening was definitely, *definitely* over. The flatness was crushing. Her brief encounter with Nikos Parakis was at an end.

The chauffeur was opening the passenger door for her and, gathering her skirts, she made herself get out. The night air seemed chilly...sobering. As if all the fizz had gone out of everything. She knew that the alcohol in her bloodstream was exacerbating her reaction, but the knowledge didn't help counter it.

Nikos followed her out, giving a brief dismissive nod to the driver, who got back into his seat at the front of the car.

Mel painted a bright smile on her face. 'Thank you for a fabulous evening,' she said. 'I had the best time ever. I hope Fiona is now duly convinced that she doesn't stand a chance with you, and focusses on her Nordic telecoms hunk instead,' she rattled out.

In a moment the evening would truly be over. Nikos would bid her goodnight and she would get the sandwich bar keys out of her bag and go inside. Nikos would get back into his chauffeur-driven car, and go off to his fancy apartment, back to his glittering, luxurious life filled with tuxedos and five-star hotels and champagne.

She'd go back to making sandwiches. And to booking a flight on a budget airline, heading for the Spanish *costas*.

She waited for the customary little thrill of anticipation that always came when she thought about her future life—but it didn't come. Instead an unexpected chill of despondency sifted through her. How could something that only a few hours ago had been her sole burning ambition now seem so...*un*burning?

Because a few hours ago I hadn't spent the evening with Nikos Parakis!

Had she sighed? She couldn't tell. Could only tell that she was making herself stretch out her hand, as if for a brisk farewell handshake. A handshake to end the evening with before she walked back into her own life.

'Thank you,' she said again. 'And goodnight.'

She would do this neatly and briskly and they would go their separate ways. He to his world, she to hers. They had been ships that had bumped briefly into each other and were now back on course to their original destinations. And that was that.

You had fun—now it's over. Accept it. Accept it graciously and go indoors.

Right now.

And stop looking at him!

But she could not stop staring at him, or gazing into his ludicrously gorgeous face and imprinting it on to her memory.

She felt her hand taken. Steeled herself to give the brisk, brief handshake that was appropriate. Nikos Parakis wasn't a date—this whole evening had been a set-up...nothing more than that. She'd done what she'd been asked to do, had had a wonderful time herself, and now it was time to bow out.

So why did she feel so damn reluctant to do so?

She could feel the blood pulsing in her veins, feel her awareness of his searing masculinity, his ludicrous good looks, as she stood on the bleak bare London pavement at two in the morning, the night air crystal in her lungs. She seemed ultra-aware of the planes and contours of his face, the dark sable of his hair, the faint aromatic scent of his skin and the shadowed darkening of his jaw.

Why, oh, why was she just stuck here, unable to tear herself away, while she felt the warm, strong pressure of his hand taking hers? He was folding his other hand around hers as well, drawing her with effortless strength a little closer to him. Looking down at her, his long-lashed eyes holding hers just as effortlessly as she gazed helplessly up at him.

'Goodnight—and thank you for coming with me this evening.' There was a husk in his voice that belied the prosaic words.

Her hand was still enclosed in his and she was standing closer to him now. So close that she could feel her breasts straining, as if she wanted only to press forward, to bind herself against the strong column of his body. She longed to feel that sheathed muscled strength against the pliant wand of her own body, to lift her mouth to his and wind her fingers up into the base of his neck, draw that sculpted mouth down upon hers...

It shook her...the intensity of the urge to do so. Like a slow-motion film running inside her head, she felt her brain try to reason her way out of it. Out of the urge to reach for him, to kiss him...

It had been so, so long since she had kissed a man— any man at all. And longer still since she had given free rein to the physical impulse of intimacy. Jak had left for Africa long ago, and since then there had been only a few perfunctory dates, snatched before caring for her grandfather had become all-consuming.

And now here she was, gazing up at a man who was

the most achingly seductive man she'd ever encountered, wanting only to feel his mouth on hers, his arms
around her.

As if he heard her body call to him he bent his head
to catch her lips, and his mouth was as soft as velvet.
As sensuous as silk.

Dissolving her completely.

She moved against him and felt her breasts crushed
against his torso, that strong wall of steely muscle. Her
other hand lost its grip on her evening bag. It fell to the
ground, letting her freed hand do what it so wanted to
do—to slide beneath the fall of his tuxedo jacket, her
fingers gliding around his back, strong and smooth and
so, so warm to her touch.

Her eyes fluttered shut as she gave herself to a slow,
velvet kiss that seemed to lift her right off her feet, that
absorbed every part of her consciousness. Gave herself
to the sensuous caress of his lips on hers. Assured, expert, arousing...he knew exactly how to glide and tease
and coax her lips to part for his, to deepen the kiss with
skilled touch until he had everything of her he sought.

How long he kissed her for she didn't know. She
knew only that her fingers were pressing into his
back, holding him fast against her, and that her hand,
still crushed in his, was being held in the valley of
her breasts, whose peaks were taut against his chest
and beneath whose surface her heart was beating like
a soaring bird.

His mouth let hers go and he was looking down
at her—at her parted lips, her dazed eyes, her heated
cheeks. His face was unreadable, but there was a shadow
somewhere deep in the dark pools of his eyes... There
were words he wanted to speak—but he kept silent...

How long she stood there, just gazing at him, overwhelmed by his kiss, she couldn't tell. Something ran between them. She could not quite tell what, but she would not let herself read that wordless message. Would only, with a breathy little catch in her throat, step back from him, separating their bodies.

Then, with a jerky movement, she bent her knees and scooped up her evening bag, made her fingers open the clasp, extract her keys. She focussed on movement, focussed on stepping towards the door, unlocking it, opening it. When she was half inside, she turned.

He hadn't moved. He was still standing there, watching her. Behind him, his car purred silently at the kerb. It would take him back to his world and she would never see him again.

There was a sensation of tightness in her chest suddenly, as if breathing were impossible. Her eyes rested on his outline one last time.

'Goodbye, Nikos,' she heard her own voice say, softly now. Then she turned away, heading towards the back room.

The evening was over now. Quite over.

Outside on the bare pavement Nikos went on standing for a while, motionless. Then, with a sudden jerky movement of his body, he turned on his heel and got back into the car.

It moved off along the deserted road.

In his head, that wordless message hung.

It was a message he did not want to hear—never wanted to hear. Had spent his life blocking out.

A message that challenged all the precepts by which he lived his life.

CHAPTER FIVE

WITH A YAWN, Mel set the tap running to fill the hot water urn and started her routine preparations for opening up the sandwich bar. But her thoughts were a million miles away, remembering everything about the evening before. It filled her head as if she were there again, reliving it all. Reliving, most of all, that melting goodnight kiss from Nikos...

For a moment—just a moment—she experienced again that sense of questioning wonder she'd felt as they'd gazed into each other's eyes. Then, with an impatient shake of her head, she shook it from her. For three long years she'd had no romance in her life at all—no wonder she was feeling overwhelmed, having been kissed by an expert kisser like Nikos Parakis!

Her mouth gave a wry little twist. He'd have acquired that expertise by kissing scores of females in his time. Kissing, romancing and moving on. Keeping his romances simple—transient. Avoiding serious relationships.

Well, she could sympathise. Right now, with freedom beckoning, that was the way *she* saw things, too—no commitments, no complications. Just enjoying light-hearted, fun-time romance if it came her way...

She made a face as she set croissants to warm. Well,

it wasn't going to come her way courtesy of Nikos Parakis—that was for sure. He'd kissed her goodnight and headed back to his own life. He hadn't wanted anything more of her than that single evening.

She paused in the act of reaching for a packet of butter from the fridge.

What if he had? What if he'd asked for more?

Like feathers sifting through her mind, she felt again that moment when he'd finished kissing her—when they'd parted but had still simply been looking at each other, their eyes meeting. A message had passed between them…

A message she hadn't been able to read—*wouldn't* read.

She shook her head, clearing the memory. What did it matter anyway? Nikos was out of her life as swiftly as he'd come into it and she wasn't going to be seeing him again. That melting goodnight kiss was what she'd remember of him—the final icing on the *amuse-bouche* that had been the evening she'd spent with him.

And in the meantime she had a loaf of bread to butter.

Nikos was running. Running fast. But not fast enough. He upped the speed on the treadmill, his feet pounding more rapidly as his pace picked up. But he still could not outrun the memory in his head.

The memory of his kiss with Mel.

It kept replaying in his head…the feel of her mouth, soft and sensuous beneath his, that taste of heady sweetness in her lips…and it was still doing so now, back in Athens, over a week later. He was still remembering the words he had not spoken—the words he'd come so close, so very, *very* close to murmuring to her…

Don't let the evening end now—come back with me— come back and stay the night with me...

But, as they'd drawn apart, as he'd finally relinquished her mouth, her soft, slender body still half embraced by his, she'd gazed up at him with that helpless, dazed expression in her beautiful eyes and the words had died on his lips. That wordless, unspoken message that had flowed between them had been silenced.

He knew why.

To have invited her to stay the night with him would not have been fair to her. He did not know her well enough to risk it—after such intimacy she might expect of him what he could not, *would* not give. He could not offer her anything other than a brief, fleeting romance.

Oh, he was no Lothario, getting a malign pleasure out of rejecting women after they'd fallen for him. He would far rather they *didn't* fall for him. Far rather they shared his terms of engagement. His short-term view.

Because the best relationships were short-term ones. He had ample personal evidence of that. His jaw tightened. And ample evidence that those who did not adhere to that view ended up in a mess. A mess that had fallout for others, as well.

Like children.

He knew only too well, with bitterly earned self-knowledge, that was why he did not risk long-term relationships. Because they could become a trap—a trap to be sprung, confining people in relationships that became prisons. Prisons they were incapable of leaving.

His expression darkened. That was what had happened to his parents. Locked in a destructive relationship that neither of them would or could relinquish. A macabre, vicious dance he'd had to watch as a boy. Still had to watch whenever he spent time with them and saw them gouging at each other like two wounded, snarling animals trapped in the same locked enclosure.

Why the hell they hadn't divorced years ago he could never fathom. Whenever he'd challenged either of them as to why they'd stuck together they'd both turned to him and said, 'But it was for *your* sake we stayed together. So you would have a stable home. There's nothing worse than a child growing up in a broken home.'

He gave a choke of bitter laughter now. If that had been their reasoning, he wasn't grateful for it. He'd headed for university in the USA with relief, then found his own apartment once he'd graduated and come back to take his place at the family bank.

He was still trying to avoid their recriminations about each other. He left them to it. Heard them out, but did not really listen. Got back to his own life as quickly as he could. Took up with women who would never be like his mother, would never turn him into a man like his father. Women who understood, right from the off, that while he spent time with them he would be devoted to them—but when that time ended he'd simply move on. When it came to the goodbye kiss, goodbye was what it meant.

Would Mel have understood that?

That was what he did not know—had not risked asking that night in London. Which was why he had to put that evening behind him, that kiss behind him—why he had to stop remembering it.

But that was what seemed so impossible, however hard he tried.

The treadmill slowed, coming to the end of its programme, and he stepped off, heading for the weights. But even as he pumped his muscles he could still feel the memory of Mel in his arms, feel the sensual power of that amazing kiss. It haunted him wherever he went, whatever he did.

Back at work, he made yet another determined effort to move on. Keeping busy must surely help. His diary for today was full, and tomorrow morning he was flying to Geneva. Then he was scheduled for Frankfurt, and after that there was some banking conference somewhere he was due to speak at. Where was it being held? Somewhere long-haul, he thought. New York? Atlanta? Toronto? Was that it?

But as he clicked on the link a completely different venue sprang up on his screen.

Bermuda.

An offshore banking haven, only a couple of hours' flight off the US East Coast, and best of all a subtropical paradise. He'd been before on business, but always on his own. The beautiful island just cried out for spending more time there, R&R—and not on his own...

The thought was in his head before he could stop it. Instantly he sought to eject it, delete it, but it was no good. It was there, indelible, right at the front of his mind. He knew exactly who should be with him on such a break—exactly who it was he wanted there.

Instantly he summoned all the arguments against it—the arguments that had stopped him whispering the words he'd wanted to whisper to Mel—but they were being drowned out. Drowned out by a cacophony of counterarguments.

She longs to go abroad—anywhere in the world. Bermuda would be perfect for her. It's not the kind of place she'd ever get to on her own—not the place for budget backpacking tourists—but with me it would be possible. I could show her a place she would otherwise never see.

It was a brilliant idea—just brilliant. And now it was in his head he could not obliterate it. It would not be silenced.

He stared out over his office, his thoughts churning. Overwhelming him with their power.

Why do I assume she would want more from me than a simple holiday romance? Why do I fear she would want something deeper, more lasting? Why not ask her and see? After all, she told me she wanted to see the world, travel everywhere—does that sound like a woman who wants to tie me down or get involved in a heavy relationship?

Even as he thought it alarm snatched at him. When had she said she was leaving London? Setting off on her travels? She might already be in Spain for all he knew.

The thought was like a blow. If she were gone, how would he ever find her?

She could disappear completely and I'd have no clue where she was!

Without realising it he'd reached for his phone. Urgency impelled him, overriding everything else. Only one thing filled his head—Mel, as she'd been that evening, so fantastically beautiful, so soft and ardent in his arms, the sweetness of her mouth, the honey of her lips.

I won't let her disappear from my life. Not without seeing whether I can't persuade her to come with me!

His secretary answered the phone instantly. Mood soaring, he gave her his instructions.

'Cancel Geneva and Frankfurt. Book me to London tomorrow instead.'

'Sarrie, here are the accounts for while you were away. I think they're looking quite good. I made a few tweaks to the menu, and tried out a few new things. I think they've worked.'

She'd added more boxed salads for diet-conscious customers, and sourced a scrumptious organic carrot cake for when they fell off their diets, keeping careful tabs on costs, sales and profits.

A sudden shaft of memory assailed her—of how she'd spun that impressive-sounding line about FMCG customer-facing research at that charity do, surrounded by all those high-flying career women. She hadn't meant it seriously…it had just been to amuse Nikos…

No. No thinking about Nikos.

No remembering that evening. And no remembering that devastating goodnight kiss.

This time tomorrow I'll be in Spain, and if I want romance I'll set my cap at some sultry Spaniard. That will take my mind off Nikos Parakis.

It had better.

Because so far nothing was taking her mind off him and everything was reminding her of him—even packing for Spain. When she'd refolded the evening gown she'd worn for him memories had rushed back into her head—memories of how he'd gazed at her when she'd glided up to him in the hotel, how he'd smiled at her, how at the end of that wonderful, fabulous evening he'd taken her into his arms to kiss her…

Stop it. Just…stop it. It's over, he's gone, and he's not coming back into your life.

That was what she had to remember. That was what she had to think about.

Not about the way he kissed me…turning me inside out and back again…

Most of all not wishing there had been more than just a single kiss…

If he'd kissed me again—swept me off my feet—if I'd gone with him—

No, she must not think of that—definitely, *definitely* not that!

And anyway—she dropped a clanging reality check down through her hectic thoughts—he *hadn't* kissed her again, had he? And there'd been no sweeping her off her feet, had there? No, he'd just kissed her goodnight and gone. The evening had ended and her brief, fleeting acquaintance with Nikos Parakis had ended, too.

Time for her to move on. To put Nikos Parakis out of her head for once and for all.

She heard the shop door open and, leaving Sarrie in the back room with the accounts and her packed suitcase, went through to serve their latest customer.

And froze.

'Hello, Mel,' said Nikos Parakis.

Emotions surged within her. Mixed emotions. Fighting each other. One emotion—the rational one that went with her head, that went with her packed suitcase, her airline ticket to Spain and her new life—was dismay. Just as she was finally on the point of leaving London, making a new start, putting him and their brief, intoxicating encounter behind her, *this* had to happen.

But that emotion didn't last. Couldn't last. It was flooded out by a far more vivid one.

Nikos was here—right here—just the other side of the counter, half a metre away and exactly as she remembered him. Tall, ludicrously, ridiculously good-looking, with his sable hair and his olive skin, and his eyes…oh, his eyes…all dark and velvety, with lashes you could sweep floors with. And the look in them was turning her stomach inside out.

The rush of emotion was unstoppable, palpable. Her face lit. She couldn't stop it.

'*Nikos!*'

The long lashes swept down over his dark, gold-flecked eyes. 'I'm glad you're still here,' he said.

She bit her lip. 'I'm flying off tomorrow morning,' she said. Did her voice sound breathless? She didn't know—didn't care. Knew only that her heart had started pounding, her pulse racing. Nikos Parakis—no longer just a memory of a fabulous evening, a goodnight kiss to remember all her life—was here, now, right in front of her in real, glorious flesh.

He smiled, and the tug of his mouth was doing things to Mel's stomach that it shouldn't—but did all the same.

'Then I've arrived just in time,' he said.

She stared. 'In time for what?' she asked automatically.

He changed his stance, became relaxed somehow. It made Mel aware all over again of the long, lean length of him, of the way the jacket of his suit fitted like a glove across his shoulders, the way his silver-buckled leather belt snaked around his narrow hips, the way the pristine white of his shirt moulded the strong wall of his chest. She felt the force of his physical impact on her assailing her senses like an onslaught of potent awareness...

'In time to ask you something,' he elucidated.

There was an expression in his face now that Mel could not read. Truth to tell, she could not do anything other than gaze at him, feeling her heart-rate soaring in her chest.

The intensity of emotion inside her kicked once more. He was speaking again. Saying something that knocked the breath out of her. Stilled her completely.

'Would you...?' Nikos said, the eyes resting on her veiled suddenly, she realised, even though they met hers. 'Would you consider a…detour…before you head for Spain?'

There was a husk in his voice as he put the question to her. The question he'd cancelled his engagements for, flown to London for. He'd driven straight here from Heathrow and walked into Sarrie's Sarnies to invite this fantastically beautiful woman, whom he could not get out of his head, to come to Bermuda with him.

Seeing her again, now, he wanted to hear only one answer to the question. Just seeing her in the flesh had slammed the truth of that into him with the full force of a tangible impact. He'd felt a kick go through him—a stab of exultation. Desire had coursed through him like a flash flood.

Would she accept what he was offering her? Share a few weeks with him, no more than that, before she headed off on her travels and they went their separate ways?

His eyes rested on her and his brow quirked. She was looking at him. Was it with a wary expression in her luminous blue eyes?

'I don't understand…' she said.

He elucidated. 'I'm due to speak at a conference in Bermuda next week. I was wondering…' his long lashes dipped over his eyes as he studied her reaction '…if you'd like to come with me?'

She didn't answer—not for a full second. She'd gone very still. Then her expression changed.

'Don't tell me Fiona Pellingham is going to the conference, as well?' she asked.

Mel's voice was dry. But her emotions, whirling around inside her, were not dry at all—they felt as if they were in a spin cycle, like turbulent laundry. Was

Nikos *really* standing there asking her to go to Bermuda with him?

He shook his head immediately. 'Nothing like that,' he assured her. His expression changed. 'This is just for you and me.'

She was staring at him still. 'Why?' she asked.

'Why?' he echoed. Then he smiled. 'Because, Mel Cooper, I can't get you out of my head—that's why. One kiss,' he told her, 'was not enough.' He paused. '*Will* you come with me?'

He could see her face working—see the emotions flitting through her gaze. He took a breath. Before this went further he had to speak—anything else would not be fair.

'A holiday, Mel—that's what I'm asking you to share with me. A holiday—fun, relaxation, good times. With each other. A few weeks in the sun. On a beautiful island which,' he said, 'I suspect is probably not on your itinerary but which, I do promise you, you *will* enjoy.' He paused. 'What do you say?' he asked.

She was silent still.

His voice changed. 'Mel, we can't deny the charge between us—it would be pointless to do so. So let's not deny it. Let's have some time with each other—a holiday—and then…' He took a breath. 'Then you go off on your travels, as you planned, and I… Well, I go back to banking. Nothing more demanding than that.'

He watched her take it in. It had been uncomfortable to spell it out, but he knew he'd had to. He wanted no deceit, no false expectations, no hope for anything more of himself than he could give her.

She'd gone very still again. She was resting her eyes on him, but not, he thought, really seeing him. It was as if she were absorbing what he'd said to her. What was behind what he'd said.

He fixed his eyes on her, waiting for her answer. Then she spoke. There was less strain in her voice now, but her tone was serious for all that.

She lifted her chin, looked right at him. 'Nikos... You gave me, without doubt, the most glamorous evening of my life. And you don't need me to tell you that that goodnight kiss would have won you a gold medal.'

The slightest tinge of humour infused her voice, and then it was gone again.

'But I really, *really* should say no to you now. It's the sensible thing to do. To say thanks, but I'm going to Spain tomorrow. I'm never going to see you again.' She closed her eyes for a moment, then opened them again. '*That's* what I've got to say to you.'

She meant it—meant every word. Of course she did. It was the only sensible thing to do. Nikos Parakis was temptation personified. How could he not be? But even with what he was offering her—a no-strings romance, a couple of weeks in the sun, in a place she'd never be likely to go to herself—she felt the ripple of danger go through her.

She'd melted like chocolate at a single kiss—what would she be like after a fortnight with him? And after a lot more than a kiss.

You melted because you haven't been kissed for years and the man who kissed you is a world champion kisser!

Her thoughts ran on...hectic, whirling around in her head...

Don't you deserve something like this? Something thrilling and wonderful and fantastic, with a man like Nikos? He's offering you exactly what you want now—a carefree, no-strings holiday romance. A few weeks of bliss and fun. Fabulous while it lasts—and unregretted when it's over.

His expression had changed. She didn't quite know how, but it had. He was looking at her still, but there was a glint in his eye—a gleam of humour and of expectation.

'And are you?' he asked. His voice was limpid, his eyes lucent. '*Are* you going to say that? Say goodbye to me again?'

Mel looked at him. Heard the confidence in his voice and knew the reason for it. Knew, too, what the sensible answer was—but why *should* she be sensible now? Her life was her own from now on—she could make decisions that maybe weren't sensible, but so what? *So what?*

A flutter of emotion went through her. She took it for excitement. Seized it. If a single evening with Nikos had been an *amuse-bouche* before the banquet that was to be her new life of freedom, and his melting kiss the icing on that *amuse-bouche*, then a holiday with him—and all that entailed—would be the most fabulous *entrée*.

The flutter of emotion came again. Oh, it was definitely excitement. And why not?

Nikos was a gorgeously irresistible male—why should she resist him? They both wanted the same thing from each other—so why not take it?

He was quirking an eyebrow at her, waiting for her answer. A smile was curving his mouth…his eyes glinted in the sunlight.

She took a breath, lifted her chin. *Yes*, she would do it!

Her mouth split into a dazzling smile.

'So,' she said, 'when are we going?'

CHAPTER SIX

'I CAN SEE IT,' Mel's voice sounded excitedly. 'There—just coming into view!'

Nikos leant sideways in his seat, peering out of the porthole. 'So it is,' he said.

Mel gazed entranced as the deep cobalt sea beneath changed colour to a paler blue. The curving shoreline was fringed with a clear reef line, changing the colour of the sea yet again, turquoise in the lee of the little bays, with foam from the ocean swell catching on the rocks of the reef.

Could this really be happening? Could she really be gazing out over the western Atlantic, flying in a plane and descending to a subtropical, reef-fringed island far below?

She'd barely had time to say goodbye to Sarrie, her face flushed and her eyes as bright as sapphires with excitement as she'd seized what Nikos was offering her. And now here she was, Nikos beside her, as the plane descended to the tiny island below.

She could see houses and gardens and palm trees now, closer and closer, and then there was the tarmac of the runway and they were touching down.

'We're here!' she exclaimed.

Nikos grinned. She was reacting like a kid, but he

could see why. Hell, he was pretty damn ecstatic himself. Here he was, his hopes utterly fulfilled, with Mel beside him, coming away on holiday with him—and she was everything he'd remembered about her. Even more beautiful… His gaze softened as it skimmed over her.

Deplaning was swift, and so was Immigration.

'It's so *British*,' exclaimed Mel, looking at the large portrait of the Queen that graced the immigration hall.

'It *is* British.' Nikos smiled. 'An Overseas Territory—the last outpost of Empire. But most visitors are Americans, because it's so close to the Atlantic seaboard. You can get here from New York in a couple of hours—short enough for a weekend.'

When they left the small airport building a chauffeured car was waiting for them. Mel spent the journey with her face pressed almost to the window, gazing at the scenery as they left the airport and started to head south.

'It will take a good forty minutes or so to reach the hotel, and we should get a good sunset there—the hotel is right on the beach,' Nikos told her.

He was thinking ahead rapidly. With jet lag, and Mel not being used to dealing with it, she would probably need an early night. He'd booked adjoining rooms at the hotel because he didn't want to rush her, or appear crass, and he knew—reluctantly—that a romantic evening tonight might not be on the cards.

He continued with his tour-guide speech. 'We're bypassing the capital, Hamilton, although the old capital, St George's, is a must-see while we're here. It's one of the oldest European settlements in the New World. Most of the island south of Hamilton is covered by villas, as the land mass is so small here, but there are botanical gardens, and a few small agricultural plots. Of all things, Bermuda is famous for its onions.'

Mel laughed. 'It's all so incredibly *pretty*,' she said, gazing out over the stone-built houses, many of them painted in pastel shades of pink and pale green and yellow, set in lush tropical gardens with palm trees, hibiscus and vivid bougainvillaea. 'The houses have funny roofs—sort of stepped tiles.'

'It's to catch rainwater and channel it down into underground cisterns,' Nikos explained. 'There are no rivers here—the island is volcanic in origin, and the big harbours to the west are the remnants of an ancient caldera. So rainwater is essential. The island is lush, but the rainy season is only for a few months in the winter. Overall, the island is very fortunate. There are occasional hurricanes, but by and large it's clement all year round.'

Mel glanced back at him. 'Shakespeare is said to have used it as his inspiration for Prospero's magical island in *The Tempest*,' she said.

'Maybe he did. It was known to Europeans by then, and St George's was settled early in the seventeenth century. It was a dangerous place, though—the surrounding reefs are full of the wrecks of unfortunate ships.' He quirked an eyebrow at Mel. 'Do you fancy trying diving while we're here?'

Her eyes widened. '*Can* we?'

His smile warm and embracing. 'Mel, we can do anything and everything while we're here. This is our time together, and I really, *really* want you to have the time of your life.'

He did, too. It would be a joy and a pleasure to give her the holiday of her dreams—and he would take pleasure in *her* pleasure. Take pleasure—oh, such pleasure—in her altogether. Mel in his arms, his embrace, his bed...

Right now, life was very sweet indeed. This was set to be a great holiday—

'Oh, this is so *beautiful*.'

Mel's exclamation came from the heart. Sun was pouring over the breakfast terrace at the hotel, dazzling on the azure sea beyond. Palm trees waved in a deliciously light breeze, and canvas parasols shaded the breakfast tables.

Mel gazed about her, fizzing with excitement and wonder. Bermuda, the fabulous hotel, the glittering blue sea, the heat, the palm trees, the vivid exotic flowers tumbling everywhere over walls, the glimpse of a sparkling marble pool a few steps beyond the terrace—they were all real. No dream, no mere photo in a travel brochure, but all, *all* real.

And real, too, was the man standing beside her. Inside the fizzing champagne of excitement in her veins she felt her blood gave a kick, shooting adrenaline through her system.

Nikos was right here, beside her. She'd grabbed the strong, warm hand he'd held out to her and run off with him, winging across the wide Atlantic to land here, on this beautiful, gorgeous island in the sun.

She turned and grinned at him. 'It's just absolutely fantastic!' she exclaimed. 'I can't believe I'm really here.'

'Believe it,' Nikos assured her, his eyes smiling as they rested on her. Drinking her in.

Her long golden hair was caught back with a scarf, but the breeze was blowing it into a halo around her head, and her face was alight with pleasure as she gazed around, eyes wide. His breath caught at her beauty.

And the hotel was perfect—tucked away on a promontory overlooking the long, reef-fringed south shore beaches to the east and a calm, sheltered bay to the west, perfect for sailing. The accommodation was low-rise, pastel-painted cottage-style rooms, all with sea views.

'Is this where your banking conference is going to be?' she asked Nikos.

Nikos shook his head. 'No, that's taking place at one of the much larger, more modern hotels, closer to the airport.' He reached for the jug of chilled orange juice that a server had just placed on the table with a smile. 'I'll take a taxi there on the day I have to speak.' He glanced at Mel. 'Do you want to come along?'

She gave him a mischievous smile. 'I wouldn't miss it for the world,' she assured him. 'Seeing you in your natural environment.'

He made a slight face. 'My natural environment?' he echoed. 'Is that what you think?'

She looked at him. 'I don't know,' she answered. 'I don't know you well enough, Nikos.'

Her voice was sober suddenly, her expression uncertain. Did she *want* to know Nikos? Did it matter to her who he was? Wasn't he just a fantastic, gorgeous man whose company she enjoyed and who could melt her with a kiss? Wasn't that enough for her?

He reached across the table with his hand, just grazing her cheek with his fingers. The gesture was soft, fleeting. Reassuring.

'There is no rush,' he said. 'We're here to enjoy ourselves.'

The smile was in his eyes, on his lips. She nodded, relaxing now. He saw it, and was glad.

'Speaking of which...' He took a mouthful of freshly squeezed orange juice. 'What do you want to do after breakfast?'

Mel's answer was immediate. 'Hit the beach!' she enthused. 'I can't wait to get into that water. It's like something out of a travel brochure.'

'Great idea,' he agreed. 'The beach it is. We'll laze the morning away—and very possibly the afternoon, too.'

Which was exactly what they did.

After a leisurely breakfast, with Nikos regaling Mel with all he knew about Bermuda, they went back to their rooms to change into beach clothes. As she let herself into her room Mel knew she was grateful to Nikos for being sufficiently sensitive to the impulsive nature of their holiday together and reserving separate rooms.

Yes, she knew—oh, she most *certainly* knew—what she had committed herself to, but to have arrived last evening, jet-lagged as she'd been, and to have been thrust into the immediate intimacy of sharing a room— a bed—would have been too...too... Well, too awkward, really.

And definitely too rushed. When they came together—a little frisson of excitement shimmered through her at the thought—it would be when they were relaxed, comfortable with each other, and with a wonderful sense of anticipation having been built up during the day and heightened to heady passion in the evening...

Then he'll take me in his arms, kiss me as he kissed me before. But this time...oh, this time it will not be goodbye...it will be the very opposite.

Nikos and me, embracing, entwining, his mouth on

mine, his body clasped by mine, only passion and desire between us...

She gave her head a quick shake to clear the image.

Yes, well, that was for later. For now, she had to change into her new swimsuit, which would be christened in the turquoise waters of Bermuda.

Another little quiver of disbelief went through her as yet again the realisation of just where she was impacted. How absolutely gorgeous it all was.

Hurriedly she slipped into her swimsuit, pulling a long, loose, semi-transparent cover-up over her head and pushing her feet into flip-flops. She grabbed her beach bag and headed outdoors via the private patio, separated from Nikos's by a low grey stone wall that could be hopped over in a second.

Nikos was already waiting for her, lounging back in one of the terrace chairs at the little dining set provided. He got to his feet, and Mel's breath caught.

Board shorts in deep cobalt-blue hugged lean hips, and his torso was moulded by every square centimetre of a white short-sleeved top bearing a fashionable surfing logo. And he was sporting wrap-around sunglasses that made her want to drop her jaw gormlessly open and gaze at him.

It took a moment for her to realise that he was returning her stare. She couldn't see his eyes behind the opaque sunglasses, but that was just as well, part of her registered. The other part was trying hard to ignore the insistent fact that beneath the veiling of her cover-up and the sheer material of her swimsuit her breasts were shamelessly engorged, following an instinct that was as powerful as it was primeval...

I want him.

The stark, visceral words sounded in her head almost audibly as she stood, rooted to the spot.

'Ready for a hard day's beach-lounging?' Nikos smiled at her, the corners of his sculpted mouth crinkling.

Mel took a breath. 'All set,' she said with determined lightness, and they headed down the path that would take them to the beach below.

A line of white sunbeds had been set out along the pale sand that was already too hot to walk on. A beach steward ushered them to a pair with a little table in between them, a parasol overhead for shade, and towels draped over the foam mattresses, with more neatly folded at the end of each lounger. They settled themselves down, and the steward enquired if they would like refreshments from the beach bistro.

'OJ and sparkling mineral water, please.'

Mel smiled. How blissful just to give a request like that and know that two minutes later it would be served to her as she relaxed back on her lounger, gazing out over the sea, feeling the warmth of the day like a cocoon around her.

'This,' she announced feelingly, 'is absolute bliss.'

'No question,' agreed Nikos.

He reached across the space between their respective sunbeds and took her hand. It was an instinctive gesture, and he was hardly aware of doing it—except that the moment his fingers wound into her hers he knew it felt right.

Mel turned to look at him, then smiled. A warm, wide smile that seemed to encapsulate everything about what they had done—run off here, to this beautiful island in the sun, to have time to themselves, to have the affair that both of them wanted to have. He knew that with absolute certainty.

He gave a deep sigh of contentment and looked out to sea again. Beside him, Mel gave an echoing sigh—and then a wry little laugh.

'It's just so gorgeous,' she said, 'to lie here with absolutely nothing to do except relax on the beach. I feel utterly idle.'

Nikos turned his head to glance at her. 'That's the general idea of a holiday,' he said, amused.

She gave a semi-shrug. 'Well, I'm not used to holidays.' She glanced away, towards the brilliant azure sea glinting in the morning sunshine, then back to Nikos. 'I've waited just *so* long to start my real life—to travel as I've longed to do—that now I am I can't quite believe it. I keep feeling I should be working.'

The focus of Nikos's gaze sharpened slightly. 'Tell me,' he asked, 'why do you feel so strongly that you should be working all the time?'

He cocked an interrogative eyebrow at her, but his voice was merely mildly curious.

Mel's expression changed. Became thoughtful. But also, Nikos thought assessingly, became guarded.

'Habit, really, I suppose. Like I say, I'm not used to holidays. Not used to having time off.'

'I seem to remember you said you did waitressing in the evenings, after the sandwich bar had closed?' Nikos recalled. 'How long did you keep that kind of double shift going? It can burn you out in the end, you know.'

He sounded sympathetic, but Mel shook her head. 'Oh, no, that wasn't a problem. I was working for myself—building up my bank balance to fund my getaway. It was a joy to work, to be honest, in comparison with looking after my grandfather. *That* was—' She broke off, not finishing.

What word would describe that period of her life? Only one—*torment*. Absolute torment...

Torment to watch the grandfather she'd loved so much become more and more frail, in body and mind. Torment to be the only person who could look after him—the only person he wanted to look after him—so that she could never have a break or even the slightest amount of time to herself.

He was looking at her curiously now, and she wished she'd kept her mouth shut.

'Was he ill?' Nikos asked. Again, his voice was sympathetic.

'Yes,' she said tightly. 'His mind went.'

'Ah... Dementia can be very hard,' acknowledged Nikos.

A kind of choke sounded in Mel's voice as she answered. 'I was raised by my grandfather after my parents died when I was very little—they were killed in a car crash. My grandfather took me in to stop me going into care. That's why, when he needed care himself, it was my...my turn to look after *him*, really.'

Her voice was tight, suppressed. She didn't want to talk about this—didn't want to think about it, didn't want to remember.

Nikos was frowning. 'Surely you didn't have to cope single-handed? There must have been help available? Professional carers on call?'

Mel swallowed. Yes, there had been help—up to a point. That hadn't been the problem. It was hard to explain—and she didn't want to. Yet somehow, for some reason—maybe it was her release, finally, from the long years of caged confinement at her grandfather's side as he made the slow, dreadful descent into dementia and eventual death—she heard the words burst from her.

'He didn't want anyone else.'

Her voice was low, the stress in it audible to Nikos.

'He only ever wanted me—all the time. He couldn't even bear to let me out of his sight, and he used to follow me around or get distressed and agitated if I just went into another room, let alone tried to go out of the house. He'd wander around at night—and of course that meant that I couldn't sleep either…not with him awake and wandering like that…'

Her voice was shaking now, but still words poured out of her, after all the months and years of watching her grandfather sink lower and lower still.

'It's what the dementia did to him. He was lost in his dark, confused mind, and I was the only thing in it he recognised—the only thing he wanted, the only thing he clung to. If I tried to get a carer from an agency to sit with him he'd yell at her, and he'd only calm down when I was back in the room again. It was pitiful to see. So no matter how exhausting it was, I just couldn't abandon him—not to outside carers—nor put him into a nursing home. How *could* I? He was the only person in the world I loved—the only person in the world who loved *me*—and I was absolutely adamant I would take care of him to the end.'

Her expression was tormented.

Nikos's voice was quiet, sombre. 'But the end did come?' he said.

She swallowed the hard, painful lump in her throat. 'It went on for three years,' she said, her voice hollow. 'And by the time the end came he didn't know me—didn't know anyone. I could only be relieved—dreadful though it is to say it—that he was finally able to leave his stricken body and mind.'

She shut her eyes, guilt heavy in her heart.

'I'd started to long for the end to come—for his sake, and for mine, too. Because death would finally release him—' She swallowed again, her voice stretched like wire. 'And it would finally release me, too…let me claim my own life back again.'

She fell silent—horrified by what had poured out of her, shutting her eyes against the memory of it, haunted by the guilt that assailed her. And yet she remembered that terrible, silent cry of anguish at the captivity his illness had held her in.

She'd never said anything of her anguish before—never said anything of those heartbreakingly difficult, impossible years she'd spent as her grandfather's carer. And yet here she was, spilling her heart to a man who was little more than a stranger still…

Beside her, Nikos had stilled as he heard her out. Now, slowly, instinctively, he reached across for the hand that she was clenching and unclenching on her chest as she relived those tormented years she'd spent at her ailing grandfather's side. She felt his palm close over her fist, stilling her.

'You did your very best for him,' he said quietly. 'You stayed with him to the end.'

He took a breath, the tenor of his voice changing.

'And now you deserve this time of freedom from care and responsibility.' His voice warmed and he squeezed her hand lightly, then let it go. 'You deserve the most fantastic holiday I can give you.'

She felt her anguish ease, and took a long, deep breath before opening her eyes to look at him.

'Thank you,' she said, and her eyes were saying more than mere words could.

For a moment their gazes held, and then Nikos deliberately lightened the mood. He wanted to see her happy again.

'Tell me,' he said, 'would you like to take a boat out sometime?'

Her expression lit as she followed his cue. Glad to do so. Glad to move away from the long, dreadful years that were gone now. Her grandfather, she hoped, was in a far better place, reunited with his long-lost family. And she was free to live her own life, making her own way in the world, enjoying her precious, fleeting youth untrammelled by cares and responsibilities. Revelling in all the new experiences she could.

Like skimming across the brilliantly azure sea that lay before her.

'Yes, please! I've never been on a boat.'

His eyebrows rose. 'Never?'

She shook her head. 'No, never,' she confirmed. 'My grandfather didn't like the water. It was as much as he'd do to go on seaside holidays when I was a child. He would sit in his deckchair, in long trousers and a long-sleeved shirt, and wish he were elsewhere while I played, merrily building sandcastles and splashing around in the freezing cold English Channel.'

She spoke easily now, far preferring to remember happy times with her grandfather. Then her expression changed again.

'When I was older I used to gaze across the water and long to see what was on the other side.' She smiled. 'And now I know. It's *this*—this blissful, gorgeous place.'

Instinctively she reached for his hand, squeezing it lightly. 'Thank you,' she said. 'Thank you for bringing me here. I shall treasure the memory of this all my life!'

Nikos lifted her hand and grazed her knuckles lightly,

so lightly, with his mouth. Little flurries of electricity raced along her skin at his touch.

'It is my pleasure to bring you here,' he said, the husk audible in his voice.

Mel could feel desire pool in her stomach. Then, with a little laugh, she dropped his hand.

'I can't resist the water any more,' she cried, and got to her feet. She peeled off her cover-up and glanced down at Nikos. 'Last one in is a sissy!' she taunted wickedly, and hared across the hot sand to where the azure water was lapping at the beach.

She ran right into the water, which was blissfully warm to the skin, and plunged into its crystal-clear embrace. Behind her she heard a heavier splash, and then Nikos was there, too, grinning and diving into the deeper sea like a dolphin, surfacing again with his sable hair slicked back and water glistening like diamonds all over his broad muscled shoulders and torso.

'Not going to get your hair wet, then?'

It was his turn to taunt, and with a toss of her locks Mel mimicked his dive into the gently mounded swell and swam underwater, to emerge further out to sea, almost out of her depth. She trod water while Nikos caught up with her in two powerful strokes.

'This is glorious!' she cried exuberantly. 'The water's so warm it's like a bath!'

His grin answered hers and he dived again. Exuberance filled him as he surfaced for air some way yet further out. Mel swam to him and her eyelashes were glistening with diamond drops of water. Her slicked-back hair emphasised the perfection of her sculpted features. How incredibly beautiful she looked.

Without conscious thought, he caught her shoulders and pressed a swift, salty kiss on her mouth. Not with passion or desire, but simply because—well, because he wanted to. It lasted only a second and then he was away again, powering through the blue waters of the warm sea.

Mel came racing after him in the same exuberant mood. That sudden salty kiss had meant nothing—and everything. A joyous salutation to the playful pleasure of being in the warm, embracing sea, bathed in glorious bright sunshine, with fresh air and water spray and absolutely nothing to do except enjoy themselves. And enjoy each other...

The afternoon passed in as leisurely and lazy a fashion as the morning until, with the sun lowering, they made their way up the winding paths towards their rooms. Mel's skin felt warm and salty, and a sense of well-being filled her.

'A good first day?' Nikos asked.

'Oh, yes,' Mel assured him. She gave a sigh of happiness and went on walking. The day might be over but—a little thrill went through her—the night was only just beginning...

And what the night would bring was what she longed for: Nikos in her passionate embrace.

The little thrill went through her again.

The process of transforming herself from beach babe to evening goddess took Mel some considerable time.

'Take as long as you want,' Nikos had assured her, his eyes glinting. 'I know it will be worth the wait.'

Nearly ninety minutes later she checked herself out in front of the long mirror on the wardrobe door.

As she did so a memory fused in her head of the way she'd tried to inspect her appearance in Sarrie's back room, with nothing more than a hand mirror.

I had no idea that I'd be here only a couple of weeks later—here with the man I was meeting up with that night!

A sense of wonder went through her. And as she let her gaze settle on her reflection she felt wonder turn to gladness. She looked *good*.

She was wearing another find from her charity shop hunts—this time a sleeveless fine cotton ankle-length dress in a warm vermilion print, with a scoop neck that hinted at a décolletage without being obvious. Her jewellery was a simple gold chain, hoop earrings and a matching bangle, her footwear low-heeled strappy sandals comfortable to walk in but more elegant than flip-flops. She'd left her hair loose, held back off her face with a narrow hairband, so that it fell in waves around her shoulders. Her make-up was light, for she knew her face was flushed from the sun, protected though her skin had been all day.

Slipping her arms into the loose, evening jacket that went with the dress and picking up her bag, she headed out—ready for the evening ahead. Ready for all the evening would bring her—and the night that would follow...

When Nikos opened the door of his room to her soft knocking the blaze in his eyes told her that her efforts had been more than worthwhile, and she felt the blood surge in her veins. Her pulse quickened with her body's response to him as she gazed in appreciation at his tall, lean figure, clad now in long linen chinos and an open-necked cotton shirt.

He guided her forward through the warm, balmy night, along the oleander-bordered path up towards the main section of the hotel, where they would be dining, and she could catch the spiced warmth of his aftershave mingling with the floral tones of her own perfume, giving her a quivering awareness of his presence at her side.

The same awareness of him remained with her all through dinner, which was taken on the same terrace where they had breakfasted. The tables were now decked in linen, adorned with tropical flowers, with silverware catching the candlelight and the light from the torches set around the perimeter.

She felt as light as gossamer, floating in a haze of happiness to be here now, like this, with this man, in this gorgeous place, eating food that was as delicious as it was rare, beautifully arrayed on the plate, melting in her mouth, washed down with crisp, cold wine.

What they talked about she hardly knew. It was the same kind of easy, casual chat they had indulged in all day. About Bermuda, the sights they would see as they continued their stay, its history... They talked about films they had seen and enjoyed, about travel, all the places Nikos had been to that Mel was eager to hear about. Easy, relaxed, companionable. As if they had known each other for ever.

Yet underneath, beneath their relaxed conversation, Mel knew that a current was running between them. Another conversation was taking place and it was signalled to her in every raised beat of her heart, every swift mingling of their eyes, every movement of his strong, well-shaped hands as he ate or lifted his glass.

She knew she was keeping that conversation beneath the surface of her consciousness—knew that it was necessary to do so. For otherwise she would not be able to function in this social space. Yet the knowledge that it was shared with him, that just as she was constantly aware of *his* physical presence—the way his open-necked white shirt framed the strong column of his neck, the way his turned-back cuffs emphasised the leanness of his wrists—so he was aware of her, too—of *her* physical being. The way the candlelight hollowed the contours of her throat, caught the glint of gold in her earrings, burnished the echoing gold of her hair.

They were both aware of the courtship being conducted—silently, continually, seductively. Aware, with a growing, subtle assurance, of just how that courtship must find its completion…that night.

And so it did.

As they rose from the table eventually—the candles burnt low, almost the only couple left out on the terrace—without thinking she slipped her hand into Nikos's as they strolled back into the interior of the hotel. It seemed the right thing to do. The obvious thing.

His warm, strong fingers closed around hers and it felt right, so right, to let it happen. To walk beside him, closer this time, her shoulder sometimes brushing against his, her skirts fluttering around her legs, catching against him. From inside the hotel they could hear the low sound of a piano being played somewhere.

'Would you like another coffee? Or a drink in the lounge?'

'Only if you would,' she answered, glancing at him.

His eyes caught hers. 'You know what I want,' he murmured. 'And it isn't to be found in the piano lounge.'

There was humour in his expression, in his eyes. But his voice, when he spoke next, was serious.

'Is it what *you* want, Mel? Tell me truly. If it isn't, then you must say now. Because, to be honest…'

Now the humour was back again, and she could hear a touch of self-mockery, too, and was warmed by it.

'I'm not sure I've got the strength of mind or character to walk you back to your room and not come in with you—'

She glanced up at him, with a similar self-mocking wry humour in her own eyes. 'I'm not sure I've got the strength of mind or character to stop you coming in,' she told him. 'In fact…' She bit her lip. 'I strongly suspect I'd yank you inside my room even if you were being strong-minded—'

He gave a low laugh, and Mel could hear the relief in it. The satisfaction. She gave an answering laugh as they headed off through the gardens, back towards their rooms, towards what both of them knew would happen now…

There was a pool of darkness nearby, where the light of the low-set lamps that lined the stone pathway did not reach, and she felt him draw her into it with a swift, decisive movement. His hand tightened on hers and the other drew her round to face him. He was close… so close to her.

She felt her heart give a little leap and that electric current came again, sizzling through her body. She could not see his expression, but she knew what it was… what it must be…what hers must be. He was dim against the night, against the stars…

Unconsciously, instinctively, she lifted her face to his. His free hand slid to cup her throat, to tilt her face higher. She felt the smooth, gliding pressure of his fingers—their warmth, their sensuous touch. Felt her heart beating wildly now, her breath catch.

He was standing with his legs slightly apart, a dominating male stance, one hand still gripping hers, the other fastened to her with a strong, sensuous hold, the pad of his thumb on the delicate line of her jaw.

His long dark lashes dipped low over his eyes, glint-

ing in the starlight. 'Well, if that's your attitude...' his
voice was low and husky, and it made her bones weaken
'...I'd better not disappoint you, had I?'

For a moment—just a moment—he delayed, and
the pad of his thumb moved to her mouth, gliding leisurely across her lips. Her bones weakened further and
her pulse quickened. With every fibre of her being she
wanted him to kiss her...wanted to feel the warm pressure of his mouth...wanted the sweet taste of him...

'Nikos...'

She must have murmured his name, must have half
closed her eyes, waiting, longing for his mouth to swoop
and descend, to take hers in its silken touch.

His fingers wound in hers and his thumb slipped
away now, his fingers touching at her throat, her jaw,
gentling, caressing. And then finally...finally...his
mouth descended to hers. Kissing her softly, sweetly,
sensuously.

Endlessly.

She folded into him. A gesture as natural, as instinctive as the way her mouth opened to his. She wanted to
feel the fullness of his kiss, the full bliss of it, as every
part of her body dissolved into it.

Beneath the glint and glitter of the stars, in the soft,
warm air, with the perfume of the night-scented flowers the susurration of the cicadas all around, his kiss
went on and on. Claiming her, arousing her, calling
forth from her all that she would bestow upon him that
night, telling of all that he would give to her.

When his lips finally left hers she felt as if she was
still in his embrace—as if she were floating inches off
the ground and as if her heart were soaring around like
a fluttering bird. He led her down the path to his room
and then they were inside, in the cool, air-conditioned

dimness. No light was needed—only the pale glow from the phosphorescence of the open sea beyond the windows.

He took her into his arms again, slipping his hands around her slender waist, cradling her supple spine as she leant into him, offering him her mouth…herself.

His kiss deepened, seeking all that it could find, and she offered all that she could give, her lips moving beneath his, her mouth opening to his in a rush of sweet, sensuous bliss. She could feel the blood surge in her veins, the heat fan out across her body, as she leant into him to taste, and take, and give, and yield.

She could feel him gliding the jacket from her shoulders, his warm hands slipping down her bared arms, and then she was pulling away from him slightly, and in a single fluid movement lifting the dress from her body, shaking her hair free of its band, giving a glorious, breathless laugh of pleasure, of anticipation.

As Nikos's eyes feasted on her she stood there, clad only in bra and panties, and a heady recklessness consumed her. Wordlessly she slipped the buttons of his shirt, easing her hands across the strong, warm column of his body. He caught her hands, his breath a rasp in his throat, and then he was folding her arms gently back, using the same movement to haul her against him, his mouth dipping to the soft, ripe swell of her breasts.

She gave a little gasp, feeling her nipples engorged against the straining satin of her bra. A low laugh came from him as his hands glided up the contour of her spine to unfasten the hooks that were keeping his mouth from what it sought to find. She felt her bra fall to the ground, felt his lips nuzzle at her bared breasts delicately, sensually, teasing and tasting until she gasped again in the sheer, trembling pleasure of it.

Her head fell back, her eyes fluttering closed, and an unconscious movement to lift her breasts to him overwhelmed her. A growl of satisfaction came from him and then he was scooping her up, lifting her as if she were a featherweight, carrying her across to the wide, waiting bed and lowering her down upon it.

She lay upon its surface, breasts still engorged and peaked, her eyes wide as she gazed up at him. Swiftly he discarded his own clothes, and then, with a groan, came down upon her. His weight crushed her, but she gloried in it—gloried in his questing mouth that now roamed her body, his hands likewise, exploring and caressing and arousing such that if the world had caught fire that very hour she would have burned in the flames that were licking through her now.

Her breath quickened, her pulse racing as she clutched his strong, hard shoulders, feeling her body yielding to him, feeling his glorious, piercing possession of her that felt so right, so incredibly, wonderfully right, nestling in the welcoming cradle of her hips. She felt the fire intensify within her, consuming her, until in a final conflagration she heard herself cry out, heard his answering cry, and felt a pleasure so intense it filled her entire being, shuddering through her, shaking and possessing her, on and on and on...

Until the quietness came.

Their bodies slaked, they held each other with slackened gentleness, beside each other, loose-limbed, embracing.

She sought his mouth. A gentle, peaceful kiss. He kissed her back, then grazed her forehead with a kiss, as well. His eyes were soft in the dim light.

There were no words—there did not need to be—only the gradual slowing of their racing hearts, their hectic pulse subsiding now. He drew her to him, his arms around her, hers around him, and with a little sigh she felt sleep take them.

CHAPTER SEVEN

'So, what would you like to do today? Anything on Bermuda you haven't seen yet?'

Nikos smiled encouragingly at Mel. They were breakfasting on Nikos's patio, gazing out over the aquamarine waters of the bay, as calm as a mill pond at this time of day. Breakfasting together like this had become the rule in the days since they'd arrived, after rising in a leisurely fashion, both of them having awoken to yet more arousal after a night of searing passion.

Hastily she reached for her coffee, hoping it might cool her suddenly heated cheeks. Time to focus on the day's activities—yet another wonderful, blissful day of self-indulgent holidaymaking.

In the week they'd already spent on Bermuda they'd covered nearly all the sights.

They'd toured the historic Nelson's Dockyard at the far west of the island, where British men-of-war had once dropped anchor, and which now welcomed massive cruise ships, disgorging their passengers to throng the myriad little cafés and craft shops.

They'd taken the ferry from the dockyard across to the island's bay-lapped capital, Hamilton, lunching on the sea front and exploring the shops. They'd gone to the old capital of St George's in the north of the island, with its white-painted little houses, art galleries, churches and museums.

And they'd been out to sea—Nikos had taken her sailing in the bay and further afield, and they'd enjoyed a sunset champagne dinner on a sleek motor yacht chartered to sail them around the island. He'd hired a dive boat, which had hovered over the reef for Nikos to dive with the instructor, leaving Mel content to snorkel on the surface, glimpsing long-sunk wrecks rich with darting fish, and the scary but thankfully harmless purple jellyfish that trailed long tentacles in the water deep below her.

Mel had wanted to see and do everything, had been excited and thrilled by even the simplest things— whether it was wandering through the beautiful gardens around the hotel, or pausing for coffee at a little Bermudian coffee shop overlooking one of the beautiful pink sand beaches. She was just revelling in being in this beautiful place, in the company of this fabulous man...

This is the most fantastic holiday romance that anyone could ever wish for.

Again she felt heat fan her cheeks. Nikos was so sensual and passionate a lover she was blown away by it. Never had she realised how incredible it could be when two people gave themselves to each other up to the very hilt of passion. How in the moment of union their bodies could pulse with an intensity, an explosion of sensual overload that wrung from her a response she had never felt before.

Jak had been a careful lover, and her memories of him were fond and grateful, but Nikos—ah, Nikos was in a league of his own. All the promise…all the shimmering awareness of the irrepressible physical attraction that had flared between them right from their first intemperate encounter…had exploded on their first night together. And now, night after night, when he took her in his arms, skilfully caressed her body to melting, she felt transported to a level of sensual satiation she had never known existed. And it was Nikos who took her there…

Will there ever be anyone in my life like him again?

The question was in her head before she could stop it. And so was the answer.

How could there be? How could there be anyone like him again—how could there be a time like this ever again in her life?

A little quiver went through her, but she silenced it. She had come away with Nikos with her eyes open—knowing he wanted only a brief, passionate affair and nothing more. Knowing that that was exactly what she wanted, too. A fabulous, gorgeous, breathtaking *entrée* in the feast of freedom that was to be her new independent life.

Nikos was for the wonderful, wonderful *now*, and that was how she was going to enjoy him—how she was going to enjoy their time together, night after night, day after day.

Speaking of days…

'We still haven't done the Crystal Caves,' she said. 'Could we visit them today?'

'Why not?' Nikos answered with lazy complaisance. 'We can take the hotel launch around to Hamilton, do a spot of shopping, have lunch and take a taxi on to the caves.'

His eyes rested on her warmly. How right he'd been

not to let her fly off to Spain and disappear on her travels without him. Instead he'd brought her here, romanced her and made love to her, and he was with her day in, day out.

Satisfaction filled him—more than satisfaction.

Contentment.

He wondered at it. It just seemed to be so easy to be with Mel—so natural, so absolutely effortless. Conversation was easy with her. They still sparked off each other, just as they had right from the first, but now it was always humorous, easygoing, mutually teasing each other, but with a smile. And it was as easy *not* to talk as it was to talk. They could wander or lie on sun loungers or watch the sunset in happy silence.

Yes, being with Mel just seemed to…*work*. That was the only way he could explain it.

Not that he wanted to analyse it, or find words to describe being with her. No, all he wanted to do was enjoy this time with her. Enjoy it to the full. In bed and out.

And that gave him an idea—a very good one, now he came to think of it.

He glanced at his watch. 'I think the hotel launch leaves every hour to make the crossing to Hamilton. Do you want to make the next one? Or would you prefer to skip it and we could take an early siesta, maybe?'

He threw her an encouraging look.

Mel gave a splutter of laughter. She knew perfectly well what he meant. And sleep would *not* be involved!

'Early siesta? It's barely gone ten in the morning!' She got to her feet, stooping to whisper to him, 'You're insatiable—you know that? Honestly. Come on.' Her voice was bracing now. 'If we get going we can get the next launch.'

'So keen to go shopping in Hamilton?' It was Nikos's turn to sound teasing.

She gave another splutter of laughter. 'No. I don't need a thing—my bathroom's chock-full of complimentary toiletries.'

Nikos smiled indulgently. 'So easily pleased...' he said fondly.

'Well, I am!' Mel riposted. 'Everything...' she waved her arms expansively, taking in the whole resort and the island it was on '...is brilliant.' She turned a warm gaze on Nikos. 'And *you're* the most brilliant of all.'

He reached to stroke her sun-warmed bare arm. 'That's the right answer,' he laughed. 'I am *definitely* more brilliant than complimentary hotel toiletries,' he finished feelingly. 'And if you really, *really* insist...' he gave an exaggerated sigh '...I shall deprive myself of our...er...siesta...until after we get back from these Crystal Caves you're determined to drag me to.'

'Oh, you'll *love* them,' she assured him with a playful thump. 'They're a marvel of nature, the guidebook says. Limestone caves with pools and walkways all illuminated like something out of a fairy tale. What's more...' she glanced at him with a determined look in her eyes '...we won't need a taxi—you can get there by bus from Hamilton. I think we should do that—I'd love to see Nikos Parakis on a humble bus.'

He laughed, and they finished off their breakfast companionably, in harmony with each other and with the day ahead.

Gratitude for all that she had been given ran through Mel like circling water. So much. This fabulous place, this fabulous time—and this fabulous man who had given it to her and was sharing it with her.

* * *

The Crystal Caves were as breathtaking as she'd hoped from their description in the guidebook, and after their visit they headed back to their hotel and some time on the beach.

As the sun lowered, though, Nikos got to his feet.

'You stay on down here for a while,' he told her. 'I need to head back to my room—check over my speech for tomorrow.'

'Oh, my goodness—is it the conference already?' Mel asked, surprised.

'I'm afraid so. But, like I've said, I'm only putting in a single day there. Then we can get on with the remainder of our holiday.' He smiled.

Her eyes followed him as he made his way along the beach. A little frown furrowed her brow. Halfway—they were halfway through their holiday already. Nikos had said 'the remainder'—that was a word that had a tolling bell in it, pointing towards the end. The end of their time together. The end of their romance.

She felt a little clenching of her stomach.

The end.

Her gaze slipped away, over the sea beyond. Her frown deepened, shadowing her eyes. Theirs was a holiday romance—a brief, gorgeous fling—and holidays always came to an end. But it would also mean a start to her independent travels—her footloose, fancy-free wandering—going where she wanted, when she wanted, tied to no one and bound to nobody...

Not even Nikos.

It's what I want—what I've planned. What I've always intended.

The reminder sounded in her head—resolutely. Determinedly. Silencing anything else that might be trying to be heard.

* * *

The conference hall was packed with delegates in business suits, and Mel had to squeeze into a space at the rear. But from there she still had a good view of Nikos on the podium. But it wasn't his discourse on sovereign debt or optimal fiscal policy that held her gaze. Oh, no.

It was the way his bespoke tailored business suit moulded every long, lean line of his fit, hard body. The way his long-fingered hands gestured at the complex graphs displayed on the screen behind him. The way his expression—focussed, incisive, authoritative, as befitted a man who had responsibilities she could not dream of—would suddenly give a hint...just a hint...of the humour that could flash out so beguilingly.

So she sat and gazed, spellbound and riveted, until his Q&A session had ended and the audience was dispersing for lunch.

She didn't join him—this was his world, not hers—instead making her way to the poolside bistro. The area was busy, but after her lunch she found an empty sun lounger in the shade and settled down to leaf through a magazine, content to while away the afternoon until Nikos was finished with the conference.

A voice nearby interrupted her. 'Hi—didn't I see you in the conference hall before lunch?'

The American-accented voice was female, and friendly, and it came from the next lounger along. Mel looked towards the woman, taking in an attractive bikini-clad brunette, a few years older than her, with an extremely chic hairstyle and full eye make-up.

The woman smiled. 'Wasn't that last speaker something? The foreign guy with his own bank—total *dish*!' Her dark eyes sparkled appreciatively.

There was an air of shared conspiracy, an invitation to agree with her, and Mel found herself smiling in wry agreement.

Taking it as consent to keep chatting, the woman continued. 'Are you here as a delegate yourself? Or a spouse?'

'Well, not a spouse—just…um…a "plus one." I guess you'd call it,' she answered, not sure whether she should mention that she was the 'plus one' of the 'dish'… 'What about you?' she asked politely.

'Oh, my husband's a banker,' the woman said. 'John Friedman of Friedman Hoffhaus,' she added, looking expectantly at Mel.

Mel gave an apologetic shake of her head. 'I'm afraid I'm very ignorant of the banking world,' she answered.

'Oh—so who are you the "plus one" of?' the woman asked curiously.

Mel's expression changed again. 'Well, actually… um…it's the "dish",' she said apologetically.

Immediately the woman's eyes sparkled. 'No *way*! My, oh, my—you are one lucky, *lucky* lady! Mind you…' she nodded in tribute to Mel's blonde beauty '…I can see how you pulled him. The thing is, though,' she went on airily, 'how are you gonna *keep* him? Men that rich *and* young *and* good-looking are hard to hog-tie. You're going to have to have a watertight "get him to the altar" strategy to be his *permanent* "plus one"!'

Mel looked uncomfortable, not wanting to elaborate to a stranger on the fact that she and Nikos were simply here together on holiday and weren't an established couple—and that she was in no need of a strategy to 'hog-tie' him.

Not that Nikos was the kind of man to get hog-tied anyway.

For an instant so brief it wasn't measurable in time

a flicker of emotion went through her—but what that emotion was she could not tell. Did not want to…

The other woman was talking again. 'Maybe you'll find yourself pregnant,' she said, and now there was an openly conspiratorial look in her eye. 'That's what happened to me—worked like a dream.'

She glanced towards the shallow end of the pool, where Mel could see a preschooler splashing about, with a young woman—presumably his nanny—playing with him.

Mel was thankfully spared the necessity of responding to such an untoward comment by a server gliding by, offering coffee. She took one, and so did the woman, who now introduced herself as Nyree, eliciting a reciprocal if somewhat reluctant response from Mel.

She was relieved when Nyree Friedman changed the subject to that of shopping opportunities, for which she considered Bermuda inadequate, which led to her regaling Mel with the delights of New York for that purpose, and giving a little cry of disbelief when she discovered that Mel had never been there.

'Oh, but you *must*! Tell the dish you absolutely *have* to go from here,' she urged.

Not waiting for an answer, she chattered on, and Mel was happy enough to leave her to it. Nyree Friedman was chatty and convivial, but Mel had to conclude she was something of an airhead.

She didn't seem to be much of a devoted mother, either, for she was perfectly happy to leave her little boy's nanny to do all the entertaining of her son. Cynically, Mel presumed that the child had served his purpose in 'hog-tying' his wealthy banker father for Nyree. It was a depressing thought.

Their mostly one-sided chat about Nyree Friedman's

fashionable, affluent Manhattan lifestyle was finally brought to an end by the emergence of Nikos from the conference. He strolled up to Mel.

'There you are…' He smiled. Then his glance swept sideways to take in her partner in conversation, who had stopped mid-sentence, her eyes wide with open appreciation at the arrival of 'the dish.'

Her dark eyes sparkled. *'Hi…'* she said warmly, holding out a languid, perfectly manicured hand. 'I'm Nyree Friedman. I heard your presentation this morning—it was *fascinating*!' she breathed. Her expression was blatantly admiring.

There was a tug at the side of Nikos's mouth as he shook the extended hand—but briefly, Mel was glad to notice. No lingering contact with the attractive brunette…

'Well, I can only hope your husband was just as taken by it,' he replied drily.

Clearly, Mel realised, he knew perfectly well who Nyree Friedman's husband was—even if he'd never met his wife before.

Nyree's gaze was visibly eating Nikos up. Out of the blue Mel felt a dagger's blade of possessiveness go through her. Sharp and piercing. For an instant she wanted to grab Nikos and drag him away—and slap Nyree down at the same time, for daring to make eyes at him.

The intensity of the emotion shocked her. No *way* did she want to feel possessive about Nikos. Hadn't he told her right from the start that possessiveness was exactly what put him off a woman? The reason he'd asked her out that very first evening had been to ward off Fiona Pellingham's possessive intentions. No, possessiveness—from either of them—wasn't what their deliberately brief time together was about, she reminded herself sharply. Possessiveness had no place at all in a fun but fleeting holiday romance such as theirs was.

To her relief, Nikos's attention was back on her, and his eyes were sending a silent question that echoed his verbal one.

'I'm all done here now, Mel,' he told her. 'So if you're ready to go we can head off? Unless,' he went on politely, his glance taking in Nyree again, 'you want to stay longer?'

His tone was polite, but Mel knew he didn't want to stay on longer here at this huge, crowded hotel. He'd already told her he wasn't going to be attending the conference dinner that evening, and she'd been glad. She wasn't going to have him for much longer, and she didn't want to share him for any of that time if she didn't have to.

'No, I'm good to go,' she said. She looked across at Nyree, who was looking rueful. 'It was lovely to meet you,' she said brightly, getting to her feet.

'Well, we must meet up in New York!' Nyree said promptly. Her flirtatious gaze went back to Nikos, then changed as it moved past him. 'John,' she said imperiously, 'persuade this gorgeous man to bring his girlfriend to New York. She's never been—can you believe it?'

The man approaching was clad in a business suit, like Nikos, but he was a good twenty years older, thought Mel, and unlike Nikos very overweight.

He nodded at Nikos, then addressed Mel. 'Has my wife let you get a word in edgeways?' he asked with heavy humour. 'She does like to dominate the airwaves.'

It was said humorously, but Mel could detect underlying irritation at his wife's garrulity.

'It's been very...interesting,' Mel said politely.

John Friedman laughed again, a little too heavily, and then his attention was drawn to the small figure hurtling towards him.

'Dad! Dad!' he was calling out excitedly. 'Come in the pool!'

Mel watched him hug the pool-wet boy and ruffle his damp hair.

'I can't wait!' his father assured him. 'But I need to get changed first, OK?' His eyes went to his wife, who was still lounging back on the recliner. 'Will *you* spend any time with our son in the pool?'

There was a clear jibe in the question, and it drew an acid response from his wife.

'And wreck my hair? Don't be ridiculous. Besides, it's time for cocktails.'

'It's too early for cocktails—especially for *you*,' John Friedman said immediately. And pointedly.

Nyree's mouth thinned mutinously and it looked as if she was going to make an angry retort. To Mel's relief—for witnessing this marital acrimony was uncomfortable—Nyree's husband had turned to Nikos.

'You made a persuasive case in there,' he said, very much banker-to-banker now. 'Maybe we should discuss some potential mutual opportunities?'

'I'd be glad to,' Nikos said promptly.

'Good.' John Friedman nodded. 'Get in touch next time you're in New York.'

'Make it *soon*!' Nyree enthused, her gaze fastening greedily on Nikos again.

Nikos gave a non-committal smile and took Mel's hand, squeezing it meaningfully. He wanted out, she knew. And so did she. For all their superficial politeness, the atmosphere was uncomfortable, and the tension between Nyree and her husband was palpable. But they said goodbye politely, even though Mel could hear regret in Nyree's voice, and saw her eyes linger on Nikos.

As she and Nikos moved away Mel could hear Nyree start up. 'Oh, my God, John—your suit is soaking wet! Why do you let the boy maul you like that? It's ridiculous. You make far too much fuss of him.'

Her husband's voice cut across her. 'One of us needs to. You won't—so I do. I'm his father. And do you *have* to try and flirt with every man you see—even when they're obviously not interested in you?'

Mel grimaced as they got out of earshot, heading through the hotel grounds to pick up a taxi at the front. 'Eek—not a happy marriage, I think. Nor a great start for that little lad of theirs, I fear.'

There was an edge to Nikos's voice as he replied. 'No, indeed.' His expression was set. That barbed exchange they'd been witness to had been all too familiar. The sniping, the acid tones, the mutual accusations and complaints... He'd grown up with them. They weren't any easier to witness in other couples any more than between his own parents.

Mel cast him a curious, slightly guarded look. There'd been a lot in the suppressed way he'd said that.

He caught her glance and made a rueful face. 'Sorry, but they just remind me of my own parents. All smiles and bonhomie to others, but with each other constant tension and backbiting. Absolutely everything becomes a verbal skirmish.'

She gave him a sympathetic smile. 'It sounds very... wearing,' she said, trying to find a word that wasn't too intrusive into what was, she could tell, a sensitive issue for him.

He gave an unamused snort. 'That's one word for it,' he said. 'Two people locked together, hammering away at each other and making themselves and everyone else miserable.'

Mel looked concerned. 'Why on earth did they ever marry each other, your parents?' she asked.

'Would you believe it? They were infatuated with each other,' he said sardonically. 'My mother was the catch of the season—the belle of every ball—and every man was after her. She kept them all guessing, playing them off against each other, but my father ended up winning her because she was bowled over by him.'

His voice twisted.

'Then I came along and everything went pear-shaped.' He gave a hollow laugh that had no humour in it. 'My mother hated being pregnant—as she constantly tells me still—I ruined her figure, apparently. And my father stopped paying her the attention she craved. And then—worse—he felt jealous of the attention she gave me when I was little, so he started straying. That incensed my mother even more than his neglecting her, and the whole damn thing just spiralled downwards until they reached a point where they couldn't even be civil to each other.'

His mouth thinned to a tight, taut line.

'They still can't be civil to each other, all these years later. They've bad-mouthed each other for as long as I can remember. Not a good word to say about each other and expecting *me* to side with each of them. Yet they absolutely refuse to admit failure and divorce—it's beyond ghastly.'

Mel kept the sympathy in her voice. 'I used to feel very sorry for myself when I was young, not having parents, but who knows which is worse? No parents—or parents who make your life a misery growing up?'

'Yes, tough call,' acknowledged Nikos, terse now, after what he'd bitten out at length.

Where the hell had all that come from?

He found himself wondering why he'd made any reference to his bumpy childhood and warring family. It wasn't a subject he discussed with others. It was too deep, too personal. Too painful. But with Mel it had seemed...natural.

He sought for a reason for his embittered outburst.

Maybe it's because she didn't have it easy either, growing up with only a grandfather to look after her, missing a mother and father. Maybe that's why it's easy to talk to her about such things...

But he didn't want to think about his endlessly sparring parents and their utter insensitivity to anyone except themselves—their refusal to acknowledge the fact that their marriage was a failure and they should have ended it years ago. He'd washed his hands of both of them and left them to it.

Deliberately he took a deep breath to clear his clouded thoughts. He wouldn't spoil his time with Mel by thinking about his parents—let alone pouring it out to her again the way he just had. No, it was far more pleasant to know that he was here, with a woman like Mel at his side, making the most of this carefree time together.

With the conference over there was nothing more to do on the island except enjoy themselves. Revel in the passion that flamed between them and relish the absolute leisure and relaxation they had, day after golden day.

It doesn't get better than this...

The words shaped themselves inside his head and he knew them to be true. Had he ever enjoyed himself more in his life than he was doing now, with Mel? It was just so *good* being here with her. Oh, the sex was beyond fantastic—no doubt about that—and he'd always known it would be. But it was so, *so* much more than just the sex.

It's the being with her that's so good. Just every day—over meals, on the beach, sightseeing...just everything.

Right now, he thought, *I'm a happy man.*

It was a good feeling.

As they settled into the taxi, setting off for their own quiet hotel, Nikos gave a sigh of relief. 'I'm glad to get out of here,' he said. 'Now we can get back to the rest of our holiday.'

'A week to go,' said Mel lightly.

Her words drew a frown across Nikos's brow. A week—was that all? It would go by in a flash, as this last one had. His frown deepened. A week wasn't enough...

Rapidly, in his head, he ran through his diary. Was there anything critical the week after next? Offhand, he couldn't think of anything. And if there was nothing absolutely critical...

The idea that had struck him was obvious—and inspired, of all things, by the warring Friedmans.

He voiced it over dinner, having checked his online diary to confirm his assumption.

'Tell me,' he said as they settled down to their evening meal, which they were taking at the beach bistro, to refresh their spirits after the day's busyness, 'are you tempted at all by the idea of going to New York?'

Mel's face lightened. She'd been thinking along just those lines herself. Going to New York would surely be something to look forward to after this fabulous time with Nikos had ended, wouldn't it? And she needed something to look forward to...

'Oh, yes,' she said. 'It would make sense, being so close to Bermuda. If I can get a cheap flight, and find a cheap tourist hotel in Manhattan, then—'

Nikos interrupted her. 'What do you mean?' he demanded, his buoyant mood altering immediately.

There was an edge to his voice she found unaccountable. She looked at him, confused.

'Why do you talk about cheap flights and tourist hotels?' he went on, in the same frowning tone.

It was her turn to look confused. 'Well, I have to make my savings go as far as they can—'

'Not when you're with *me*,' he contradicted. His expression darkened. 'Unless for some reason you don't *want* to see New York with me?'

If she hadn't known better she might have read accusation in his voice. But accusation was so inexplicable it couldn't possibly be that.

'Nikos, that's a daft question,' she replied, in a rallying humorous tone.

But he was not mollified. 'Then what is making you talk of going there on your own?' he demanded.

She looked at him uncertainly. 'When you invited me to Bermuda, Nikos, you told me it would just be for a couple of weeks—around the conference,' she said.

He gave a dismissive shrug. 'So we make it longer. That's all. I've checked my diary and I can bring forward some meetings in New York scheduled for the following month. By extending our stay on Bermuda we can go straight from here to New York. Plus,' he finished, 'I could take up John Friedman's invitation—I dare say it would prove very useful to me.' He looked across the table. 'So, let's do it—shall we?'

His voice was expectant. But Mel's expression did not lighten in return.

'Nikos, I'm not sure it's a good idea—'

His brow darkened. 'Why?' His question was blunt.

Her eyes slid away, out over the dark expanse of water beyond the beach. She wanted to put into words her reluctance, and yet it was hard to do so. Hard because shooting through her, making a nonsense of reluctance, was an arrow of sheer exhilaration that seemed to be penetrating to her very core.

He wanted to stay longer on Bermuda, to take her to New York! Wanted to spend more time with her! Wanted not to kiss her goodbye and wave her off out of his life!

She felt the force of it—felt its power.

And it was that that gave her pause.

I came with him for a holiday romance—that's all. A couple of weeks with Nikos—a glorious, fantastic, fabulous entrée in the banquet of my new life of travelling, of freedom and self-indulgence—that was what this holiday was supposed to be. All that I planned it to be.

A holiday romance was something she could accommodate. Indeed, she'd envisaged fun-filled, light-hearted holiday romances as being an integral part of her new free life. Making up for the lost years of enforced celibacy, for the absolute lack of romance in her life while she'd cared for her grandfather.

But when did a holiday romance turn into something more?

If she let Nikos take her to New York what would come afterwards? He would still go back to Athens, wouldn't he? Still kiss her goodbye...

Her mind sheered away. She didn't want to think of that. Didn't want to think about anything except what she had now—their time together here in Bermuda. Their holiday romance...

Beautiful—and brief.

Her eyes swept back to him, found his resting on her, dark and stormy-looking.

'Why?' he asked again. 'Why is going to New York with me not a good idea?'

He would not let it go. Why was she saying such a thing? Weren't they having a fantastic time here in Bermuda? Why not keep going with it?

We're so good together.

That was what was in his head all the time. Simple, uncomplicated and true. There was no reason for her to be unenthusiastic about him going to New York with her. She wanted to go there—he wanted to go there with her. What was the problem?

He wanted her to answer so that he could dispose of her objections. But at that juncture the waiter arrived with their food, and as he left them Mel determinedly changed the subject.

He could see the ploy for what it was—a way to stop him grilling her—and he accepted it. There were more ways to persuade her than by out-arguing her...

That night, as he took her in his arms, he put into their lovemaking all the skill and expertise that lay within his command, deliberately drawing from her a consummation that left her shaking, trembling in his arms—left him shaking, trembling in hers.

Finally, sated and exhausted, they drew apart and lay beside each other, their bodies sheened with perspiration, their breathing hectic, the echoes of their shared ecstasy still burning between them. He levered himself up on his elbow, smoothing back her damp hair, gazing down into her wide eyes.

'Come to New York with me...' he whispered.

His lashes dropped over his eyes, his mouth dipped to graze her lips, parted and bee-stung from his passion.

'Come to New York with me...' he whispered again.

Surely she must be persuaded now? Surely she must not want what was between them to end before it needed to? And it did not need to—not yet. They did not have to part—they could keep going—keep going to New York and who knew how far beyond? Who knew how long this romance would last? All he knew was that he had no intention—none at all—of letting it go a single moment before he was ready.

But she didn't answer him—only let her eyes flutter shut and rolled herself into his waiting embrace. And he closed her against him, hugging her tight, so tight, against the wall of his chest.

In her head she could hear his voice—so low, so seductive, so tempting...

Come to New York with me...

In her body, deep in the core of her, she could feel the hectic pulse ebbing slowly, leaving only the incandescent afterglow of passion. She felt her breathing ease, her heated skin start to cool. But in her heart there was a tightening.

There was one thing she must say to him—only one thing. The sensible thing.

He was nuzzling at her ear, his breath warm, his touch sweet.

'Come to New York,' he murmured, coaxing and caressing. His mouth moved from the delicate lobe of her ear, grazing along the line of her jaw. 'Come to New York,' he said again.

She could feel his mouth break into a smile suddenly, and his arms tightened around her.

'Come to New York,' he said, and she could hear the

laugh in his voice. 'Because I'll go on asking you until you give in and say yes.'

He was kissing her eyelids now.

'Give in and say yes… Give in and say yes. You know you want to.'

He was laughing, and so was she, and suddenly, out of nowhere, she couldn't fight it any longer.

'*Yes!* OK—I give in! I'll come to New York with you!' Her capitulation was complete.

He gave a low, triumphant rumble and she was grinning, too, half shaking her head and then kissing him. Oh, what the hell? She hadn't been sensible at all. But she didn't care—couldn't care—not now…

Wrapping his warm, strong body against her, she wound herself tighter into his embrace. She felt a singing inside her. *She was going to New York with Nikos—* their holiday would be longer, their time together would be longer, there were still more glorious days to come.

CHAPTER EIGHT

'Is THAT YOU guzzling rum cake again?' Mel's voice was humorously indignant.

'Just testing it for quality,' Nikos assured her, licking his fingers after eating a slice of the cake that was the speciality of the island.

'Yes, well, if you test much more of it there'll be none left,' she riposted, removing the cake tin from him and placing the lid firmly back on top. 'I'll keep this in *my* room, I think.'

Nikos laughed. 'We can always go to Nelson's Harbour and restock.'

'We'll need to if you keep eating it like that.'

She dropped a kiss on his head before stepping over the dividing wall between their patios and heading indoors. Emerging again, she saw Nikos was pulling on his shirt. Despite the rum cake, his pecs and abs were still spectacularly honed.

Mel felt a ripple of desire go through her. But this wasn't the time to indulge in a siesta—not least because it was only just after breakfast and they were about to head to the beach.

As they stretched themselves out on their beach loungers, just above the tide line so that the spray from the waves breaking exuberantly into airy foam on the soft pale gold sand could cool their sun-heated bodies, lying on the beach seemed especially blissful.

But that, she knew with a squeezing of her heart, was because their days here were finally running out…

Then they'd be off to New York—for their last, final few days together.

And then goodbye…

Finally, goodbye.

Despite the heat of the beach a sudden draught of cold air seemed to be playing around her body. She fought it back.

But it's not the end of the holiday yet! I've still got time with Nikos.

And yet it was precisely the fact that she'd felt that cold draught that caused her concern.

I shouldn't be so eager to stay with him—I shouldn't be clinging to our time together like this. It isn't what I intended at all. I should be excited at the prospect of going on to see the rest of America—exploring all the places I've only ever read about or seen on films or TV. I shouldn't be wanting to go on being with Nikos all the time—I shouldn't…

But the problem was she *did* just want to go on being with Nikos. Here on Bermuda. In New York. And beyond…

For a moment she tried to force herself to imagine exploring the USA on her own—but her mind had gone blank. Beyond New York there seemed to be nothing at all…

Dismay filled her. This was not good—not good at all. For so long she'd thought and dreamt of nothing but being footloose and fancy-free, going where she wanted, when she wanted, making her own way across the world, free as a bird… Yet now there seemed to be only a blank ahead of her.

The time would soon come when they would go their separate ways—she to see the rest of America, he to head back to Athens, to his life. Their holiday together over.

The chilly draught came again.

She didn't want to think about it—didn't want to face it. Didn't want to think that in just a few days' time it would all be ending.

But what—what will be ending?

That was the question she shied away from answering.

'Mel—bad news.'

She turned abruptly, halting in the action of fastening her packed suitcase. Nikos was standing in the open French windows of her room. He was frowning, phone in hand.

'What's happened?' she asked, alarmed.

Their extended time on Bermuda had finally ended, and now they were due to head off to New York.

Mel could not deny that she'd given up on those ambivalent feelings she'd had about his determination to take her to America for a final few days together—she didn't even try. There was no point. They were going there now, and that was that. They were booked and packed. Any moment now their bags would be collected and the hotel car would take them to the airport for their late-morning flight to New York. So it was too late to question why she was so uneasy about it all—wasn't it?

'I'm going to have to change our plans,' Nikos said, his voice short. 'We have to head back to Europe. Something's cropped up and I can't get out of it—I'm really sorry.' He gave an annoyed sigh. 'New York is off the cards—I'm getting us booked on the evening flight direct to London, and then we'll need to drop down to Athens straight away...'

She was staring at him. Just staring.

He came up to her, slid his phone away and put his arms loosely around her waist.

'I'm really sorry,' he said again, apology in his eyes. 'But on the other hand...' he dropped a light kiss on her nose '...you'll get to see Athens instead of New York.'

She stepped away from him.

'Nikos—'

There was something in her voice that made him look at her.

Emotions were shooting through her like bullets. What had she just been thinking? That it was too late to be so uneasy about extending her time with Nikos yet further? Her expression twisted. Suddenly out of the blue, with a phone call that had changed.

'Nikos, I can't come to Athens with you.' The words fell from her lips.

It was his turn to stare. 'Why not?' There was blank incomprehension in his voice.

'Because...because I'm going to New York. Because seeing the USA is what I've planned to do.' She swallowed. 'I know you were going to be with me for a couple more days in New York, but I'm...I'm going on, Nikos. The way I planned.'

His face was taut. 'Change your plans. See Athens instead. Didn't you say you wanted to go "everywhere"?' he challenged. 'You haven't even set foot in Europe yet.'

She shut her eyes. She could hear a kind of drumming in her ears.

I thought I'd have a few more days with him...just a few more days...

But that wasn't going to happen. It was over—right now.

Because of course she couldn't go to Europe with him—it was out of the question. Just out of the question.

'Nikos—no. I can't.'

'You can't *what*?' he said, the words cutting into the space between them.

He could feel emotion starting to build in him, but he didn't know what it was. Knew only that the woman he wanted with him was saying she couldn't be with him...

'I can't just...just tag along with you to Athens. What *as*, for heaven's sake? Here, we've been on holiday, but if you go back to your home city—well...what will I be doing there with you? What *am* I to you there?'

How can I have nothing more than a holiday romance with you if we're not on holiday?

He was staring at her, his eyes dark, his expression darker.

She had to make him understand.

Something had changed in his eyes. 'What had you in mind?' he said.

His voice was dry. As dry as the sand in a desert.

It was her turn to stare, not understanding what he was saying—why he was saying it. Emotion was churning away inside her and she felt a sense of shock—shock that the moment she'd thought would be deferred for a few more days was upon her. Right now.

Then he was speaking.

'Mel, I was clear with you from the start, wasn't I?' she heard him say. 'Before we came here? I never fed you a line—you knew the score with me from the start. Don't expect anything more than that.'

His voice was flat, unemotional. Had she read more than he'd intended into his saying they needed to head for Athens? He hoped not—he really hoped not.

Because 'anything more' is not how I live my life. I've seen where 'more' can take people—how it can screw things up...screw people up...

His mind sheered away from familiar thoughts, familiar reactions. Things he didn't want to associate with Mel—not Mel.

I just want what we have now—because it's good... so good—and I want it to go on just the way it is. I don't see why it can't, but why can't she see that, too? Why can't we just go on the way we are? Not question things the way she's doing now?

Mel's face worked. 'Nikos, I don't expect anything more of you than what we've been having.' She swallowed, making her voice lighter. 'Which is the most fantastic holiday that anyone could ever imagine. A holiday that...' She swallowed again, and this time there seemed to be something in her throat as she did so, though she didn't know what. 'That is over,' she finished.

The expression in his eyes changed. Had she seen a flash of emotion? And if she had, what had it been?

For a moment she thought it might have been relief.

Or had it been regret?

Well, whatever it was, it didn't matter. All that mattered now was...was...

A strange, hollow sense of emptiness stretched inside her.

All that matters now is saying goodbye...

She made herself move—walk up to him, loop her arms around his neck. He was standing stock-still, all muscles tensed.

'Nikos, I have had the most fantastic time with you,'

she told him, steeling herself to say what must be said right now—days before she'd thought she would be saying it. She smiled at him, made herself smile, because smiling at this moment was suddenly very necessary to her. 'But...'

She let him go, stepped away again. She took a breath. It was painful, somehow, to draw breath in and out of her lungs, but she had to do it. Had to say goodbye to him.

'It's come to an end, Nikos,' she said. 'I'm sorry we're not getting our...our bonus time in New York, but... well...' she gave a little shrug with muscles that did not want to move '...there it is. All holidays end. So has ours.'

That was all the time they'd planned to have with each other—nothing more. So why was he glowering at her the way he was, his expression rejecting what she was saying to him?

She bit her lip, hating what was happening but knowing there was no alternative.

This has come too fast—I'm not ready...not prepared—

Out of nowhere panic boiled up in her chest, suffocating her. She had to fight it down. Had to make herself speak to him in a tone of voice that sounded reasonable.

'I'm sorry this has just happened so fast like this— but, oh, Nikos, we always knew this moment would come. Whether now or in a couple of days in New York it doesn't matter much. We mustn't make a big deal of it—it *isn't* a big deal and it mustn't become one.'

There was a plea in her voice now—even she could hear it. But who was she pleading with? Him—or herself? Well, she mustn't think about that. Mustn't think about anything except making herself reach for her nearby handbag, clutch it to her.

He was still standing there, motionless. His face was frozen, as if turned to stone.

Why is it like this? Why? It shouldn't be hard to say goodbye and get on with my own life. It just shouldn't!

'Nikos, I'm going to take the hotel shuttle to the airport—make that New York flight on my own. I know the London flight isn't till this evening, so there's no point you setting off now. And…and I don't want to say goodbye at an airport…'

I don't want to say goodbye at all.

The words were wrung from inside her, but she ignored them—she had to.

'I don't believe you're doing this.'

That deep, accented voice. But no longer flat. No longer edged. Just—harsh.

'It's for the best. It really is,' she heard herself say.

She picked up the handle of her suitcase, backing towards the door. As she yanked it open she paused. Looked at him one last time.

For some strange, inexplicable reason he looked out of focus. Blurred.

She blinked, trying to clear her vision. Trying to keep her voice the way it had to be—the only way it could be when a holiday romance came to an end. 'Have a good flight back,' she said.

She smiled. Or thought she did. She wasn't sure.

She wasn't sure of anything at all except that she had to manoeuvre her suitcase out onto the path that ran along the back of their rooms. A hotel buggy was waiting there, ready to take both of them up to the hotel for the airport shuttle. Now it would only take her.

She let her suitcase be hefted up, clambered onto the seat herself. Nerveless…numb. Her chest was bound with steel bands, her vision still blurred. The afternoon heat pressed down on her like a crushing weight.

The buggy glided off, taking her away.

In Mel's room Nikos stood very still.

The room was empty. Quite empty.

Emotion sliced through him. He stopped it. Meshed himself together again. Made himself walk towards the house phone and pick it up, speak to the front desk to request, in tones that were curter than he would normally use to a member of hotel staff, that he be booked on the London flight that evening. Then he put the phone down. Stared about him.

She'd gone. Mel had gone. That was the only thought in his head. She'd waved him goodbye and walked out.

And he couldn't believe it. Just could...not...believe it.

In the space of a few minutes he'd gone from having Mel with him to not having her.

She walked out on me. She just walked out on me!

The slicing emotion came again—vertically from the top of his head right down to his feet. Slicing him in half, as if each side of his body would keel over separately. Destroying him.

Breath ravaged his lungs as he drew air into them, hauling the two sides of his body back together again by raw strength of will. He was in shock, he knew. Recognised it with the part of his mind that was still capable of functioning, which was somewhere deep inside him, somewhere very remote, it seemed. Shock was all there was to him right now. And the disbelief that went hand in hand with it.

The ringing of the house phone made him jolt. Automatically he picked it up, listened as he was told his flight had been booked, automatically gave his mono-syllabic thanks before hanging up.

He walked out through the French windows he'd walked in through only minutes earlier. When his world had been completely different...

When Mel had been in it.

But now Mel was gone.

Oh, God, she's gone.

The emotion came again, like a sweeping knife, head to foot—and this time it severed him in two completely...

Mel was standing in bright sunlight, heat beating down on her bare head. The view was beyond all imagining.

The great chasm in the earth a few metres beyond her was a full ten miles wide at this point, she knew—one of the greatest natural wonders of the earth. But as she stood at the rim of the Grand Canyon she could not feel its grandeur, nor its wonder. All around her tourists were milling, exclaiming, taking photos, grouping and regrouping, but still she stood, gazing out over the contorted rocks that cascaded down into the belly of the earth, where far below the Colorado River snaked along the almost subterranean base of the canyon.

She was taking part in an organised day tour from Las Vegas, having flown in from Washington, where she'd gone after New York. She'd assiduously visited every landmark on the tourist trail, determined to miss absolutely nothing.

Determined to fill every moment of the day with occupation. With busyness and fulfilment.

Determined to show that she was living her life to the full, seeing the world and all its wonders as she had planned and hoped so much to do.

Determined *not* to let herself remember the brief, glorious introduction to that new life of hers that she had had courtesy of Nikos.

It had been good—brilliant—fantastic—fabulous. But it had only ever been supposed be a glittering, gorgeous introduction to her new life of hedonistic freedom after long servitude. Travelling on her own, going where she wanted when she wanted, footloose and fancy-free, answerable only to herself—that was what her new life was supposed to be about.

So she must not stand here and think of Nikos. Must not stand here and see only him in her mind's vision, not the jaw-dropping stupendous splendour of the Canyon.

And above all she must not—must not, *must not*— let that most dangerous and fatal thought creep into her head: *If only he were here with me, standing beside me now, and we were seeing all this together... If only he were seeing everything with me...*

Seeing everything with her...

If only he'd been with her in New York, seeing the sights with her as they'd planned. The Statue of Liberty, Central Park, the Empire State Building. And then in Washington, seeing all the historic monuments there, and then—oh, then the complete contrast of Las Vegas...so gaudy and garish and such ridiculous tacky *fun*!

In her head she could hear him laughing with her, murmuring to her, could feel him sweeping her into his arms, kissing her senseless and carrying her off to their bed to find passionate, burning rapture in each other's arms.

Oh, the longing for him was palpable, the yearning all-consuming. There was an ache inside her...she wanted him with her so much...

But he wasn't with her. Would never be with her again. They would never stand beside each other seeing the wonders that the world had to offer. Never sweep each other into their arms again.

So she must get used to it. Must accept it. Must simply stop letting thoughts like that into her head. Such uselessly tormenting thoughts...

She must simply go on standing there, staring blindly, vacantly out over this chasm in the earth. While inside her there seemed to be a chasm almost as vast.

CHAPTER NINE

'So, HOW WAS BERMUDA?'

It was a casually asked question, and not one that should have made Nikos tense instantly. He made himself return an equitable reply.

'Not a bad conference,' he said.

'Nice venue, too.' His acquaintance smiled. 'Did you manage to add on any holiday time?'

Somehow Nikos managed an answer, and then ruthlessly switched the subject. Whatever he talked about, it wasn't going to be his time in Bermuda. It wasn't even something he wanted to *think* about.

That desire was, of course, completely fruitless. He thought about Bermuda all the time.

And Mel. Always Mel.

Mel laughing, head thrown back, glorious blonde hair rippling. Mel gazing at him with that expression of amusement, interest—desire. Mel melting into his arms, her mouth warm and inviting, her body clinging to his, ardent and eager...

Then he would slam down the guillotine and make himself think about something else. Anything else. Anything at all.

Work was what he mainly thought about. Lived and breathed. He'd become a powerhouse of focussed, relentless dedication to the business of the bank. Deal after deal after deal. Tireless and non-stop. Rising early and working late.

He was back to working out a lot, too. Muscle mass glistened...heart and lungs purred like the engine of a high-performance car. Sinews were lean and supple like a honed athlete. It was essential to keep his body occupied.

Because his body had a mind of its own. A mind he could not allow to function—not in the slightest. A mind that made every cell in his honed, taut body crave another body—a body that was soft and satin-smooth and sensuous as silk. Flesh to his flesh...

He still wanted her.

The irony of the situation was not lost on him. He was the one who'd wanted nothing more than a temporary affair. Had wanted only a holiday romance with Mel.

But no one had said how long the holiday had to be, had they? No, they hadn't. Or *where* it had to be. It could just as easily have been here in Greece. Mel had never seen Greece, and showing her the glories of the ancient ruins, the beauty of the islands and mountains, would have entranced her.

But she'd turned it down. Turned down spending more time with him. Gone off on her travels just the way she'd always planned to.

That was what was so galling now. That the very thing that had once reassured him that she would accept the temporary nature of her romance with him was now twisting back to bite him!

Bite him hard.

The door of his office swung open and his father

strode in from his adjoining office, his expression angry, as it so often was, Nikos thought with a silent sigh.

'Do you know what your mother has done now?' his father demanded. 'She's taken herself off to Milan. She says it's because she's out of clothes—*ha!* That woman could open a fashion store with her wardrobe. But I know better. She's in a ridiculously unnecessary sulk—just because she's taken it into her stupid head that I'm having an affair with another woman.'

Nikos's mouth tightened. *Oh, great, that was all he needed.* His father sounding off to him about the latest behaviour of his wife and how it irritated him.

'And are you?' he replied bluntly.

His father waved a hand impatiently. 'Do you blame me?' he demanded, his voice aggrieved. 'Your mother's impossible! Completely impossible! She's taken off at just the most inconvenient time. We are *supposed* to be joining Demetrius Astarchis and his wife on their yacht tomorrow! Now what am I supposed to do?'

'Take your mistress instead?' his son suggested acidly.

'Don't be absurd. They're expecting your mother and me. She should be there—Demetrius and I do a valuable amount of business with each other. If nothing else, your mother should realise that the only reason she can run riot in couture houses is because of the effort I put in to keep the coffers full. She owes me *some* loyalty!'

Nikos forbore from pointing out the obvious—that loyalty was a two-way street, and keeping a mistress was not the way for his father to win his wife's. But he also knew, with weary resignation, that his mother's poisonous tongue couldn't have done a better job of driving away her husband than if she'd changed the locks on the house.

He'd never heard a conversation between them that didn't involve his mother making vicious little digs at his father all the time…or sweeping sabre strokes of bitter accusation.

He looked at his father now, standing there angrily, filled with self-righteous indignation at his wife's errant behaviour, and felt an immense exasperated irritation with them both.

'Is that what you came in to tell me?' he asked tightly, having no intention of being drawn into witnessing any further diatribes by his father against his mother.

'I wanted to check over the Hong Kong trip with you,' his father said, still ill-humoured, 'and warn you that if your mother hasn't deigned to return before you go I'll have to go and fetch her home. I'm not having her roaming around Europe, bad-mouthing me to everyone she knows. And I'm not leaving her in Milan on her own too long either—catching the eye of some predatory male!'

He gave his son a withering look.

'Not that your mother has any looks left—she's not aged well,' he said sourly. 'Which is another reason,' he finished defiantly, 'for me to find something more agreeable to look at than her crow's feet.'

Nikos forbore to add oil to burning waters by reminding his father that his mother was equally and vocally critical of her husband's jowly features and increasing paunch. Instead, all he said was, 'I've got the meetings in Hong Kong all set up. Take a look.'

He found he was glad he had a trip to the Far East coming up—it might help take his mind off his own miseries. Though it didn't do him any good to realise that he was already thinking how much he'd have loved to show Hong Kong to Mel.

We could have flown down to Malaysia after-wards, Thailand, too, and Bali—even on to Australia, maybe.

And from Australia they could have taken in New Zealand—and beyond that the verdant jewels of the South Pacific islands…

He tore his mind away. Why torment himself? Why think about holidays he would never have with Mel? All she'd wanted from him was a brief few weeks on a single island. Nothing more than that…

'Good,' his father was saying now. He glanced at his watch. 'I must go—I'm having lunch with Adela.' He paused. 'I might not be back afterwards…'

Again, Nikos deliberately said nothing.

Not even as his father headed back to his own office, adding, 'And for God's sake don't tell your mother. That's all I need.'

What you need, thought Nikos grimly, *is a divorce.*

But that wouldn't happen, he knew. His parents were locked in their bitter, destructive dance, circling round each other like snarling dogs, biting at each other constantly.

That's why I've stayed clear of long-term relation-ships. So I'll never get trapped in an ugly, destructive relationship the way my parents have.

Moodily, he jackknifed out of his chair, striding across the office to stare out over the streets of Athens below. Thoughts, dark and turbid, swirled in his mind.

He didn't want to be here, staring out over the city of his birth, working himself senseless, just to block his mind from thinking about what he *did* want—which was to be somewhere utterly different.

With Mel.

He shut his eyes, swearing fluently and silently inside his head. He was off again, thinking about Mel—wanting her…wanting her so badly it was a physical pain.

But she was gone—gone, gone, *gone*. She had walked out on him and she'd been *right* to walk out on him—that was what was so unbearable for him to face. Mel had done exactly what would have happened anyway, a few days later—ended their affair. It had been just as he had planned it to be—transient, temporary, impermanent.

Safe.

Safe from the danger he'd always feared. That one fine day he'd find himself doing what his father had just done—walking in and snapping and snarling, berating and bad-mouthing the woman he was married to.

His eyes opened again, a bleak expression in them. He could hear his father's condemnation of his mother still ringing in his ears. Together or apart, they still laid into each other, still tore each other to pieces. The venom and hostility and the sheer bloody nastiness of it all…

They couldn't be more different from the way Mel and I were together…

Into his head thronged a thousand memories—Mel laughing, smiling, teasing him with an amused, affectionate glint in her eye at his foibles—him teasing her back in the same vein,—both of them at ease with each other, companionable, comfortable, contented…

Contented.

The word shaped itself in his head. He'd used it in Bermuda—trying to find the right word to match his feelings then.

Contented.

That had been the word—the right word…

Me and Mel. Mel and me.

Because it wasn't just the passion that had seared between them—incandescent though that had been—it was more, oh, so much more than that.

His mind went to his parents. They were always complaining about each other, with lines of discontent, displeasure, disapproval around their mouths, with vicious expressions in their eyes when they spoke to each other, spoke of each other to him.

Nothing, *nothing* like the way he and Mel had been.

He felt his body tense, every honed muscle engaging, as he stared out of the window—not seeing what was beyond the glass, not seeing anything except a vision of Mel's face. Beautiful beyond all dreams, but with an expression that was far, far beyond beauty to him. She was smiling at him, with a softness in her eyes, a warmth—an affection that reached out to him and made him want to reach out to her. To cup her face and drop a kiss on the tip of her nose, then tuck her hand in his, warm and secure, and stroll with her, side by side, along the beach, chatting about this or that or nothing at all, easy and happy, *contented*, towards the setting sun...

All the days of my life...

And into his head, into his consciousness, slowly, like a swimmer emerging from a deep, deep sea, the realisation came to him.

It doesn't have to be like my parents' relationship. I don't have to think that will happen. Mel and I aren't like that. We're nothing like that. Nothing!

He could feel the thoughts shaping inside his head, borne up on the emotion rising within him. If that were so, then he could take the risk—*should* take the risk—the risk he had always feared to take. Because never had he met a woman who could take that fear from him.

As if a fog had cleared from his head, taking away the occluding mist that had clouded his vision all his life, he felt the realisation pierce him.

Mel can—Mel can lift that fear from me.

That was what he had to trust. That was what he had to believe in.

What we had was too good—far too good to let go of. Far too good to cut short, fearing what it might become in years to come. I refuse to believe that she and I would ever become like my parents. I refuse to believe that the time we had together—that brief, inadequate time—couldn't go on for much longer. Not weeks, or months—but years...

His breath seemed to still in his lungs.

All my days...

For one long, breathless moment he stood there, every muscle poised, and then, as if throwing a switch, he whirled around, turned on his heel and strode back to his desk. His eyes were alight—fired with determination, with revelation, with self-knowledge.

She might not want him—she might be halfway around the world by now—she might turn him down and spurn him, go on her laughing, footloose way, but not before he found her again and put to her the question that was searing in his head now. The question he had to know the answer to...

Snatching up the phone on his desk, he spoke to his secretary.

'Get me our security agency, please—I need to start an investigation. I need—' he took a hectic breath '—to find someone.'

The plane banked as it started its descent into Heathrow. Mel felt herself tilting, and again the sensation of nausea rose inside her. She damped it down. It had started when they'd hit a pocket of turbulence mid-Atlantic, but they would be on the tarmac soon—then she'd feel better.

Physically, at least.

Mentally, she didn't feel good in the slightest. She felt as if a pair of snakes were writhing, fighting within her—two opposing emotions, twisting and tormenting her. Her face tightened. Her features pulled taut and stark. She had an ordeal in front of her. An ordeal she didn't want but had to endure. Had to face.

This wasn't the way it was supposed to be.

A holiday romance—that was all she'd ever intended Nikos to be. A brief, glorious fling—then off on her travels as she'd planned for so long. Happy and carefree. On her own.

Travels had turned out to be nothing—to be ashes—without Nikos at her side to share them with.

It wasn't supposed to have been like that...

Missing him so much...

Missing him...missing him all the time—wherever she went, wherever she'd gone. Just wanting to be with him again. Anywhere in the world...so long as it was with him...

How could she have been so unbearably stupid as to walk out on him? He'd asked her to go with him to Athens and she'd refused.

I could have had more time...more time with him...

Yet even as the cry came silently and cruelly within her she heard her own voice answer the one inside her head—even more cruel.

How much more time? A week? A month? And then what? When the holiday romance burned itself out? When he finally didn't want you any more because all he wanted was an affair...? Nothing permanent. Nothing binding between them.

She heard again in her head his warning to her that horrible, horrible morning in Bermuda when she'd walked out and gone to the airport to fly to New York alone.

'What had you in mind? I made it clear, right from the start, that I was only talking about a few weeks together at the most...'

A hideous, hollow laugh sounded inside her. A few weeks? Oh, dear God, now she had the means to be with him, to keep him in her life, for far longer than a few weeks...

A permanent, perpetual bond between them.

Her features twisted.

No, it wasn't supposed to have been like this at all.

I wasn't supposed to fall for him.

She swallowed the nausea rising in her throat again.

I wasn't supposed to get pregnant...

CHAPTER TEN

NIKOS EXITED THE brand-new office building, heading for the car that waited for him at the kerb. He glanced up at the sky between the tall serried ranks of modern office blocks in downtown Hong Kong. The clouds had massed even more, and the humid air had a distinct chill to it. The wind was clearly rising. The local TV channel had been full of news of an impending typhoon, speculating on whether it would hit the island or not.

Back at his hotel, he noticed that the typhoon warning notice had gone up a level. His mouth set. He still had more meetings lined up, but they might have to be postponed if the weather worsened. Once a typhoon hit in force the streets would be cleared of traffic, the subway shut down and the population kept indoors until it was safe to go out again.

From his suite at the top of the towering hotel, with its view over the harbour, he could see the grey water, choppy and restless, and watched frowningly as ocean-going ships came in from the open sea beyond to seek shelter from the ferocious winds that were starting to build. The way things were going, it was more than likely his flight back to London would be cancelled.

Frustration bit at him. The last thing he wanted

was to be stuck here in Hong Kong with a typhoon threatening!

He forced himself to be rational. He'd set the security agency he used for personal protection to the task of tracking down the woman he *had* to locate—and that would take time. Even as he thought this a memory darted with piquant power—the memory of his first evening with Mel, bantering with her about how she should take a bodyguard with her on her travels to keep all predatory males away from her...

How long ago that seemed—and yet also as if it were only yesterday...

Automatically, he checked his mobile and email—still nothing from the agency. With a vocal rasp, he got stuck back into his work yet again.

Patience—that was what he needed. But he wasn't in the mood to be patient. Not in the slightest.

The tube train taking Mel into the City, towards the London offices of the Parakis Bank, was crowded and airless. She felt claustrophobic after the wide-open spaces of America, and she was dreading the ordeal that lay in front of her.

She should have phoned first, she knew, but she hadn't been able to face it. Nikos probably wasn't even in London now—why should he be? But maybe she could talk to his PA, find out where he was, how best to get in touch with him. At worst she could leave the painfully written letter she'd got in her bag. Telling him what she had to tell him...

She'd written it last night, rewriting it over and over again, trying to find the right words to tell him. The right words to tell him the wrong thing. That their holiday romance had ended in a way that neither of them could possibly have foreseen. That neither could possibly have wanted.

Yet even as she thought it she could feel emotion rising up in her—feel the conflict that had tormented her since her first shocked and disbelieving discovery of what had happened. Conflict that had never abated since—that was going round and round and round in her head, day and night.

What am I going to do? What am I going to do?

The train glided to a halt at another station and the doors slid open. More people got off. Then the doors slid shut and the train started forward again, out of the lighted platform area and back into yet another tunnel. Stop, start, stop again, start again—over and over. And still the words went round and round in her head.

What am I going to do? What am I going to do?

She was pregnant, with an unplanned baby, by a man who had only been a holiday romance. That was the stark truth of it.

It was the very last thing she had ever thought would happen.

She heard her own words, spoken so casually, so confidently, at the charity dinner Nikos had taken her to—their very first date.

'Right now, a baby is definitely not on my agenda.'

All she'd wanted was the freedom to indulge her wanderlust—finally, after so many years of looking after her grandfather. She hadn't wanted more ties, more responsibilities.

Other words cut into her mind. Not hers this time. Nikos—talking as they'd walked away from that mismatched couple at the conference hotel. Telling her bitterly how his parents had become warring enemies.

'When I came along everything went pear-shaped.'

That was what he had said. Showing her his scars—his fears. His determination never to risk what had happened to his parents happening to him.

And now, thanks to her, that was what was facing him.

Her features twisted and emotion stabbed at her like a knife…a tormenting, toxic mix of dismay, fear, doubt and fierce, primitive protectiveness…

What am I going to do? What am I going to do?

Round and round the question circled in her tired, exhausted brain, with no answer at all.

The train pulled into yet another station, and with a start Mel realised she should have changed lines at the previous one. Hastily she pushed her way off, pausing on the platform to look around for directions to the line she needed. As she was staring about the large lettering on the advert plastered to the curved wall in front of her suddenly caught her eye.

Pregnant? Unsure?
Overwhelmed? Confused?

Her gaze focussed instantly, and the words below resolved themselves into sense in her brain.

Talk to us in complete confidence for help to find your way forward.

Beneath was the name of a charity she had been vaguely familiar with in her student days, but had never had need to pay any attention to.

Until now.

She stared, repeating the words of the advert inside her head. *Unsure…overwhelmed…confused?* Dear God, she was all of those, all right. Her eyes drifted to the address given on the advert, registering that it was nearby.

Her grip tightened on her suitcase and with a jerk she started to head towards the escalators.

Oblivious of the quietly dressed man doing likewise a little way behind her...

Fifteen minutes later she was seated, hands clenched with tension, in a consulting room at the charity's walk-in offices.

'You really should take longer to think this through.' The woman talking to Mel spoke with a warm, sympathetic, but cautious tone.

'I *have* thought it through—I've thought it through over and over again...ever since I found out I was pregnant. It's the only thing I've been thinking about.'

Mel's voice was stressed. She had poured everything out, tumbled and conflicted and anguished, and the trained counsellor had listened quietly and attentively. Then she had spelt out to Mel the options that were available—the choices she could make.

As Mel had listened she had felt her heart grow heavier and heavier at the answer to the question that was tormenting her—that had tormented her ever since she had stared, disbelieving, at the blue line on the pregnancy test kit.

She looked across at the counsellor, her expression strained, but there was a resolve in her eyes that had not been there before.

'My mind is made up,' she said. 'That's my decision. My baby—my responsibility for what happens.'

She got to her feet. Once more a slight wave of nausea bit at her, and she swallowed it down.

The counsellor had stood up, too.

'I am always here,' she said, her voice kind, 'if you

feel you want to discuss this further…talk things through again.'

But Mel shook her head. 'Thank you—but, no. I know what I'm going to do.' She gave a difficult smile. 'Thank you for your time. It's been…' she took a breath '…invaluable. You've helped me to reach the answer I needed to find.'

She held out a hand, shook the counsellor's briefly and made her way back out on to the street. Her pace, as she headed off, was determined. Resolute. But her tread felt as heavy as her heart.

As she headed back to the tube station she got out the letter she'd written so painfully the night before. Tearing it in two, she dropped it in a litter bin. Then she went back down into the Underground. This time taking the direction away from the City.

Away from Nikos's offices.

There was nothing to tell him now. Nothing at all.

Her mind was clear on that.

Finally the writhing snakes that had tormented her had ceased their endless conflict.

Her baby was hers and hers alone.

And as she sat carefully down on a seat in the tube train her hand crept to her abdomen, spreading across gently. Protectively.

Nikos threw himself into his first-class seat on the plane as they boarded in Hong Kong, relief filling him. Finally he was on his way back to Europe. The typhoon had hit, just as he'd feared, and all flights had been cancelled. Now, though, the delayed flights were resuming and he was headed for London.

But he still didn't know where Mel was. His investigators had drawn a blank—and in a way he wasn't surprised. Because how *did* you locate someone who was one of thousands of tourists?

He'd told the agency about the sandwich bar she'd worked in, in case that might help. Maybe her former employer could shed some light on where she was right now? Hadn't Mel said that Sarrie was the uncle of a friend of hers?

And there was a possibility that she might be traceable by checking out the former address details of anyone with her surname who had died the previous year in North London, to see if they could locate the address of her late grandfather's house. If they could, then maybe the estate agents handling the tenancy had contact details for Mel?

With a shake of his head, Nikos waved away the glass of champagne being proffered by the stewardess in First Class, oblivious of the admiring look the attractive brunette had thrown his way. He was oblivious to all females now. Only one in the world mattered to him—the one he was trying to find—the one who was somewhere...wandering the face of the earth...

What if she's met someone else by now?

That was the fear that bit at him—gnawed at him in the night, when his body ached for Mel to be in his arms...

But he wouldn't let himself think like that—he wouldn't. He would hang on to the purpose he'd set for himself: he would find her and put to her the one thing he needed to say.

The one thing it was most vital to him that she knew.

Some twelve hours later Nikos strode out of the long-haul terminal at Heathrow. His car was humming at the kerb and he threw himself in, barely greeting his driver. Flicking open his laptop, he loaded his emails.

A surge of triumph welled in him—there was the email he'd been longing to see.

It was from his investigators and it was headed with the magic words: Subject located.

Yes! He all but punched the air even as his finger jabbed at the screen, opening the email. His eyes seized on the words and he started to read.

And then, inside his head, all hell broke loose.

Mel stepped out on to the pavement, hefting her suitcase out over the doorstop of the flat she had been staying in. It felt heavier than it had used to feel. Maybe the weakness she felt was to do with early pregnancy? Her mind was a blank—it was the only way she could keep going.

She'd booked a flight from Luton to Malaga, and now she had to get to Luton. But first she had a medical appointment. At a clinic that the counsellor at the pregnancy advisory charity had recommended to her and then made an appointment with.

The appointment letter was in her hand and she stared at the address again, trying to decide whether to take a bus or make for the Underground. The bus would be slower, but it would avoid her having to lug her suitcase down the tube station escalators.

She opted for the bus—she'd have enough suitcase-lugging to do once she got to the airport, and then at the other end in Malaga. She'd have to find somewhere to stay the night there…maybe a few days…until she could sort out accommodation and get her head around the new life she was going to make for herself.

One that was going to be so very, *very* different from what she had thought it was going to be.

But her mind was made up. There was no changing it now.

My baby—my decision. The only way it can be.

The heavy stone was still in her stomach, weighing her down, pushing the ever-present sense of nausea into her gullet. But it wasn't the physical impact of her pregnancy that was making her feel like this—feel as if she was being crushed to the ground...

She turned to start walking along the pavement towards the bus stop at the end of the road. Her feet dragged as if she was wearing shoes of lead.

The car braking sharply as it slewed towards the kerb made her head whip round. Recognition drew a gasp of disbelief from her. And then dismay.

Raw, shattering dismay.

Nikos was leaping from the car, charging up to her.

Dismay exploded in a million fragments—shot to pieces by the tidal wave of an utterly different emotion that surged across every synapse in her brain, flooding it with its totality.

Nikos! Nikos—here—in the flesh—in front of her— alive and well and *real*!

Not the hopeless memory in her head that was all he'd been these last endless weeks since she had walked away from him in Bermuda.

But real—oh, so real. How he'd suddenly appeared on the street like this she didn't know—didn't care. She knew only that a searing flash of joy was going through her.

Then that searing flash of joy was gone—shot to pieces in its turn.

Her arms were clamped in steel. His voice speared into her in fury.

'You're *not* doing it. Do you understand me? You're not doing it. I'll never let you do it. I don't care what the law says—I will *never* let you do that!'

Rage was boiling from him, burning in his eyes, and his face was twisted with anger as his words struck into her. She could only stare at him, not understanding...

Nikos saw the incomprehension in her face, layered over her shock at seeing him, and it maddened him yet more.

'How could you even *think* of it? How *could* you?'

The paper in her hand fluttered from her fingers to the ground. Automatically she tried to bend her knees to pick it up, but Nikos was still pinioning her and she couldn't move. He saw her movement and his eyes went to the letter on the ground. With a snarl he seized it himself, staring at it. His face whitened.

'*Thee mou...*' His voice was hollow. 'You're going there now—aren't you? *Aren't you?*'

From somewhere—she didn't know where—she found her voice. It was strained, as if it was being pulled unbearably tight.

'I didn't want you to know,' she said.

But it was too late now—the written proof of her medical appointment had revealed everything to him.

Another snarl broke from him. 'No! You were going ahead with it without even telling me, weren't you?'

Greek words burst from him—ugly and accusing. She didn't know what he was saying—only that it contained fury. Sickness rose in her. Dear God, she had been right in her decision not to tell him.

She made herself speak again as he stood there, the betraying letter in his hand, his face contorted with fury.

'It...it seemed the best thing to do, Nikos. I...I didn't want to involve you in any of this...'

'*Involve* me?'

He stared at her as if she'd spoken in an alien tongue.

Then a sudden, sickening realisation hit him. His hand, which had been still clamped around her arm, dropped away. He took a step back.

'Is it mine?'

Three little words—but in them a wealth of accusation. She paled, and he heard his voice going on, cutting at her with slashing words.

'It's a reasonable question to ask. After all, I picked you up easily enough, didn't I? Maybe you got a similar offer when you went off to New York without me? Maybe *he's* the guy who got you pregnant?'

She gasped as if he had struck her. *'No!'* she cried, the word tearing from her in rejection.

Emotion leapt in his eyes. 'So you admit it's mine? You admit it—and yet here you are, with the evidence of your damnable intentions in your hand, and you were going to say nothing to me—*nothing*!'

She shut her eyes, misery overwhelming her. 'I told you—I thought it would be for the best. It wasn't an easy decision, Nikos—truly it wasn't.'

More Greek broke from him, dark and furious. 'You never wanted to be pregnant, did you? Don't tell me otherwise, because I won't believe it.'

Her features convulsed. 'No—I didn't want to be pregnant,' she said, the words torn from her. 'When I realised it seemed…it seemed…'

Nikos supplied the words. 'An end to your freedom?' His voice was heavy, crushing.

'Yes. Pregnancy seemed…seemed the last thing I wanted…' She spoke faintly, as if the words could barely be spoken.

He turned her appointment letter over in his hand, his eyes never leaving her. 'And so you decided to regain your freedom,' he said, and now his words were not just heavy and crushing—they were swords, stabbing into her, strike after strike, pitiless and condemning. 'You decided to end the pregnancy.'

He saw her whiten like a sheet. The blood drained from her face. Inside him, unbearable fury lashed. Fury and something so much more.

All she wants is to get rid of the baby we created between us. It means nothing to her but a burden, a curb on her freedom!

And that was why she had bolted. Because surely she must have known that the moment he knew she was carrying his child there could be only one outcome?

For a second—just a fraction of a second—he felt his heart leap within him.

Mel—back with him. Back with him and bringing with her a gift even more precious than herself.

He felt his lungs squeezed, the air crushed from them.

But she didn't want that—didn't want him. And she had never wanted his baby.

Instead she wanted what she was set on doing now. What that starkly condemning report had told him. The report that had informed him she had been spotted entering a high street charity for a walk-in consultation.

The comment in parentheses had been unemotional.

We would advise our client that this particular charity is supportive of pro-choice options for women with unplanned pregnancies.

In a single sentence he had read heaven—and hell.

She was staring at him now, still as white as a sheet. She felt the words he'd thrown at her sear into her brain like a burning brand of accusation. Her mouth opened.

Words were desperate to take shape, to fly across the gaping space between them, to counter the dreadful accusation he had hurled at her.

'Nikos! It isn't like that. It—'

But he was cutting right across her, stopping her speaking.

'Don't try and defend it. You can call it what you like, but we both know the truth of what you are planning to do.'

The terrible words were like knives, slashing at her. She could not bear to hear them. She gave a cry, backing away as if he had struck her physically. Features convulsing, she thrust past him, out into the roadway.

She had to get away—oh, dear God, she had to get away.

There was a screech of brakes, a hideous sound of squealing rubber. And then, as if in some horror movie slow-motion, Nikos saw the car hit her…saw her frail, fragile body crumple like paper and fall to the tarmac.

CHAPTER ELEVEN

HE WAS THERE in an instant—a heartbeat. The space of time between living and dying. He was yelling—he could hear himself yelling—but it was as if it were someone else. Someone else yelling as he saw that fragile figure crumple to the ground. Someone else yelling like a madman for an ambulance.

Because he was on his knees beside her, horror in his face, his eyes, in his whole being.

Let her be alive! Dear God in heaven, let her be alive. It's all I ask—all I beg! Anything else—anything else at all—I can bear. But not that—oh, not that!

It was all that consumed him in the eternity it took for the ambulance to arrive.

She had a pulse—it was his only desperate source of hope—but she was unconscious, inert, scarcely breathing, still as white as a sheet.

I did this to her. I did it. The punishing accusation went on and on in his head.

The paramedics tended her, phoning ahead to the hospital that they were bringing her in, checking the car's driver for shock and whiplash.

Nikos piled into the ambulance with her. 'Is she going to be all right? Please God, tell me.'

But the ambulance crew were adept at tragedy, and

only gave platitudes to him. There could be no answer to that question until she was in A&E…

Time stopped…time raced. Time blurred.

When the ambulance arrived at the hospital the emergency team fell to work. Nikos hung on to the doorjamb of the resuscitation bay and prayed—prayed with all his strength.

'Just *tell* me!' He was beyond coherence.

One of the doctors looked up. 'Looks like only bruising, lacerations—no sign of internal damage…no lung damage,' he reeled off. 'One cracked rib so far. No skull trauma. Spine and limbs seem OK, though she'll need a scan to check thoroughly.

'And she's coming round…'

Nikos swayed, Greek words breaking from him in a paean of gratitude. Mel's eyes were flickering, and a low groan sounded in her throat as consciousness returned. Then, as her eyes opened fully, Nikos could see her expression change to one of anguish when she saw all the medics clustered around her.

'My baby,' she cried. '*My baby!* Oh, please—please don't let my baby be gone. Please, no—*please, no!*'

Immediately the doctor responded, laying a calming hand on her arm.

'There's no sign of a bleed,' he said. 'But we'll get you up to Obs and Gynae the moment you've had your scan and they'll check you out thoroughly. OK?'

He smiled down reassuringly and Mel's stricken gaze clung to him. Then, before Nikos's eyes, she burst into crying. 'Thank God. Oh, thank God,' he heard her say.

Over and over again…

And inside him it felt as if the world had just changed for ever.

'Thank God,' he echoed. 'Thank God.'

But it was more than the life of his unborn child he was thanking God for—so, *so* much more...

Then the emergency team were dispersing, and a nurse was left to instruct that Mel be wheeled off for a scan and then up to Obs and Gynae. Once again Nikos was prevented from accompanying her, and frustration raged within him. He needed to be with her—needed her to be with *him*.

After an age—an eternity—he was finally told that she was in Obs and Gynae and that her scans, thankfully, had all been clear. Again, Nikos gave thanks—gave thanks with all his being.

He rushed up to the obstetrics and gynaecology department, heart pounding...

There were more delays there—more being kept waiting, pacing up and down. He focussed on one thing, and one thing only—getting to Mel. And then finally—finally—he was allowed to see her.

She was in a side ward, blessedly on her own. She was conscious still, but her face was pale—apart from the grazing on her cheek from where she'd collapsed on the tarmac after the impact. Her face whitened yet more as the nurse showed him in.

He rushed up to her—then stopped dead.

The expression on her face had stopped him in his tracks. She was looking...*stricken*.

He felt a hollowing out inside him. Horror washed through him again as he saw in his head that nightmare moment when the car had struck her and she'd crumpled like paper.

Then another emotion seared through his head.

His eyes fastened on her, desperate to read in her gaze what he absolutely, totally *had* to know. He heard in his head her terrified cries down in A&E.

'My baby,' she'd cried—and he could hear her cry still. *'My baby! Oh, please—please don't let my baby be gone. Please, no—please, no!'*

Relief, profound and infinitely grateful, had ripped through him that at that moment—at that moment of extreme danger to her baby—she had realised she wanted it. Realised how precious it was. How precious *she* was.

'I nearly lost you—I nearly killed you...'

He took a jerking step towards her. Saw her expression change.

'Oh, God, Mel—I'm sorry. I'm so sorry.' The words burst from him.

Words shaped themselves on her lips. Were uttered with difficulty and strain and a terrible emptiness. 'You thought I wanted to kill my baby.'

It wasn't an accusation, only a statement. But it came from a place he didn't want to exist.

He swallowed. 'I know—I know you don't. I heard you, Mel. I heard your terror when you came round— you were terrified for your baby.'

He saw her hand move slightly, unconsciously, to lie across her abdomen. Sheltering. Protective.

Emotion stabbed within him. 'Mel, I—'

His voice was jerky, but hers cut right across it.

'How could you think that, Nikos? How *could* you?' Her eyes were piercing—accusing. Horrified.

A rasp sounded in his throat. 'You said yourself that you didn't want to be pregnant. That it would be an end to your freedom.' He took a ragged breath, memory searing through him. 'And I kept remembering how you told Fiona Pellingham that you didn't want a baby now—'

Her face worked. She acknowledged the truth of what

he'd just said—knew she had to face it. 'That was my first reaction, yes—but it wasn't the only one, Nikos. Truly it wasn't. But it was so…so complicated.'

Complicated… Such a weak, pathetic word to describe the searing clash of emotions that had consumed her as she'd stared at that thin blue line on the pregnancy testing kit.

They were there still, consuming her. Anguish churned inside her that Nikos should think…should think…

He was staring at her. 'You were on your way to an abortion clinic—I saw the appointment letter.'

Her face contorted. 'It was an antenatal appointment. That's all it was! To have a check-up before I fly to Spain tonight. How could you think it was for anything else? How *could* you?'

She took a shuddering breath.

'My old GP is miles away, and I'd have had to wait days for an appointment. So the woman at the charity made an appointment for me at a mother and baby clinic.'

He was staring at her still. Still not making sense of things. 'It's a pro-choice charity,' he said, his voice hollow. 'They arrange abortions for women who have pregnancies they don't want.'

Her features were screwed up. 'Yes, they do, Nikos. But they also help with all the other alternatives, as well. Like single-parenting—raising a baby alone.' Her expression changed again. 'How do you know I went to that charity?'

He took a deep breath. This wasn't the way he'd thought it was going to be—this moment of finding her again. Shock still reverberated through him—shock upon shock. He remembered the terror as he'd read the report that had totally changed everything—for ever. It had given him the most wonderful gift he could imagine—and threatened to tear it from him in the same moment.

Mel—carrying his child.

Mel—wanting to destroy their child…

Mel—crumpling to the ground as the car hit her, nearly destroyed by his accusation.

Cold snaked down his spine like iced water as he realised how hideously close he'd come to losing everything—everything he was most desperate to keep.

'I…I've been trying to find you. I sent investigators to search for you. They found you, finally, where you were staying—and they saw you there. I only just got their findings now—when I landed at Heathrow. I've been in Hong Kong. There was a typhoon.'

His jerky, staccato words ground to a halt.

'I've been trying to find you,' he said again.

It was, he knew, the only thing he had to say to her. Nothing else mattered—nothing at all.

Except that I've found her. That she's alive, that she carries my child!

Emotion flooded through him.

Our child—she bears our child.

Wonder and gratitude soared in him. He felt weak with it.

She was staring at him.

'You were trying to find me?' Her voice was faint.

'*Yes!* Mel—Mel, I—'

But she cut across him. 'Oh, dear God, I wish with all my heart you hadn't. I wish you'd never found me.' Her face buckled. 'Never found me and never found out about the baby.'

Her voice was anguished. Inside her that same impossible conflict of emotions was still warring, tearing her apart.

Oh, dear God, what a mess this is—what an unholy, impossible mess!

She felt again that stabbing wound, the lashing blow that she'd felt when she'd heard the full import of his words—the cruel accusation he'd hurled at her that had made her want to run, to flee straight into the path of the car that had nearly killed her—nearly killed her baby.

Nikos's baby—that I didn't want him to know about— Because if he did...

'I never meant to involve you in this, Nikos,' she said, her voice twisted, her eyes pleading.

He was staring at her again. 'What do you mean, *"involve"* me? Mel, this is *our* child. Our baby!'

How could she talk like this? Say she hadn't wanted him to know?

Words she had said earlier now registered with him— something about going to Spain, taking a flight that day...

The cold snaked down his spine again.

Had he not sent his investigators to find her she would have disappeared again.

And I'd never have known—never have known she was carrying my baby—our baby!

Fear at what had so very nearly happened gouged at him.

She was answering him—her voice low, strained.

'It doesn't have to be, Nikos. It can just be *my* baby. That's why I went to that pregnancy charity—I needed someone to talk to about not telling you about the baby. She...she helped me make my mind up. And then she went through the practicalities of raising a child single-handed, without paternal involvement, taking all the responsibility on myself.'

'*Thee mou*—why? *Why?* Why even *think* like that?' The words broke from him.

She didn't answer—couldn't. Could only press her hand against her abdomen again, feeling…needing the reassurance that her baby was safe—*safe*. The baby she would raise on her own, as she had come to realise she must. Because anything else was…impossible. Just impossible…

She felt her throat tighten. To see Nikos again—here…so real—but for him to be as far away from her as he could be…

He saw the emotion on her face. Realised what it must mean. She hadn't wanted him to know she was pregnant because she didn't want him *involved*.

Didn't want him in her life.

After all his hopes…all the hopes that had soared within him as he'd stood in his office in Athens…when he'd realised that he and Mel were nothing, *nothing* like his parents. That what they had between them could never descend into the bitter farce that was his parents' marriage.

But now his hopes were ashes in his mouth. Heaviness filled him.

She wants her freedom—the freedom she's craved for so long—the freedom she left me for and still wants.

The freedom he could not take from her—*must* not take from her.

Not even for the sake of the child she carried—*their* child. The child she wanted to raise on her own—free of him.

He sought for what he must say now. Letting go of

his hopes...letting them fall to the ground, dashed to pieces...

'You must have known...' he said, and his voice was hollow, but so, *so* careful. 'You must have known that I would...stand by you, Mel.'

He was picking his words with infinite care. All that she had said to him while they'd been together, about how precious her newly gained life of freedom was to her, came back to him like blows.

It was why she left me—to safeguard her freedom. Why she walked out on me when I wanted more of her than she wanted to give.

He would let her keep that freedom—he must. He would not try to chain her to his side in a life she did not want. If she wanted to raise their child herself he must let her—he *must*.

Whatever it cost him.

He came towards her now, took the hard chair that was near the bed and sat himself down on it. Took a deep, steadying breath in order to say what he must say now that she'd made it crystal clear that she'd never wanted to tell him about her pregnancy. Never wanted him *'involved.'* The word twisted inside him like snakes.

'You know I'll stand by you, Mel. There'll be no money worries. I'll see to everything. Look after you, whatever you choose. So you can live wherever you want—well, anywhere child-safe, obviously.'

She heard him speak, and each word was like an arrow in her. But with each word she knew irrefutably that after all her anguish and turmoil, her longings and her fears from the very moment she had seen that thin blue line on the pregnancy test, that she had done what had proved the right thing to have done. She knew she had made the right decision in determining to head for Spain, not to tell Nikos about being pregnant, not to burden him with it...

But it was too late now—he knew she carried their child. And now she would have to take the consequences of his knowledge. Protect herself from them as much as she could.

A pang went through her...

He made as if to reach for her hand, then stopped, drew back. Then he spoke again.

'I know how vital your freedom is to you, Mel. I'll protect that for you as much as I can—make as few demands on you as I can. So long as from time to time you let me...let me—'

He stopped, unable to continue.

Let me see my baby—my child. Let me see you, Mel—let me be a part of your life, however small...

He swallowed, forced himself to keep going, to keep his voice studiedly, doggedly neutral—impossible though it was to do so, when inside he was holding down with brute force what was burning inside him.

'But please, Mel, don't disappear without my knowing—that's all I ask. I have...responsibilities...for you... for the baby...'

The word tolled in her brain. *'Responsibilities...'* Yes, that was all it could be to him. He'd been angry—furious—and understandably so, when he'd thought she wanted a termination. But now that he'd realised she wanted this baby—how terrified she'd been when she'd thought she might lose it—now it was just a question of...*responsibilities*.

Responsibilities she would—*must*—keep as light as possible for him. She must assure him of that.

'I won't...impose on you, Nikos. Financially I'll be

all right. I have the rental income from my grandfather's house, and until the baby is born I can work. I'm going to base myself in Spain, probably, because I can live cheaply there. There are various child benefits I'm entitled to claim as well—that woman at the charity explained it all to me.'

'Impose?' he echoed. 'Mel, this is *my* baby you're talking about. It goes without question that I'll take care of everything.'

She shook her head violently. It hurt, but she didn't care.

'Oh, Nikos, that's why I wish to God you'd never found out. I know how scarred you are by your parents chaining themselves to each other. That you never want to run such a risk yourself. That's why you only wanted a brief romance with me. The last thing you want is to be trapped—trapped as you are now—trapped by unplanned, unwanted fatherhood. And that's why I was never going to tell you about the baby. So *you* could be free.'

Her voice was anguished, no more than a whisper now.

'If you'd never known about the baby we could both have been free of each other...'

For a moment...for an eternity...there was silence.

Then... 'Free of each other?' Nikos's echo of her words dropped like lead into the silence.

Abruptly, he let go of her hands. Pushed the chair back roughly. Got to his feet. Paced about the narrow room. Turned back to look at her. Tension radiated from him.

'Your freedom to roam the world after all those years looking after your grandfather—mine to avoid any kind of repetition of the snake pit that is my parents' marriage—is that it?'

There was something strange in his voice—something that made her stare at him. Not understanding. Not comprehending.

He didn't wait for an answer—just ploughed on. That same strange note was in his voice, the same strangeness in his face...his eyes.

'All my life I've run scared,' he said. 'Scared and, yes, *scarred*. Scarred by what I've had to witness between my warring, snarling parents. Tearing each other apart...tearing their marriage apart. And I dreaded, *dreaded* that I might end up doing the same.'

He took a breath—a shuddering breath.

'I vowed I would never run that risk. And I vowed I would never get involved with any woman who could endanger that vow. I only ever wanted temporary relationships. Nothing...deeper. Nothing...longer. Nothing longer than a holiday romance.'

There was a twist in his voice now, and it was heavy with irony. Bitter self-mockery.

'Just the way you did.' He took another breath, felt it razoring his lungs. 'We were so well suited, weren't we, Mel? In our own different ways we wanted the same thing—our freedom.'

He gazed at her—at the way she lay there, at her golden hair, her beautiful face—and a thousand memories came rushing to his head of those glorious days they'd had together—so good...so *good*.

So *right*.

And in the golden wash of those memories came knowledge, pouring like a fountain through him. Confirming—in a tidal wave of emotion—what had swept over him when he'd set out to find Mel again—to beg her to stay in his life.

He stilled. Thrust his hands deep into his trouser pockets. Stood there immobile, unreadable. Then something changed in his expression. He seemed to stand straighter—taller.

He looked at her lying there, her body ripening with their baby...their child-to-be.

'I want a new freedom,' he said. His voice was different now—resolute, adamant. 'The freedom not to be scarred by my parents' marriage—not to be fearful of repeating their mistakes. The freedom, Mel, to say finally what I have crushed down up to now, because I don't want to put on you what you do not want. You want your freedom—honoured and preserved—and I won't try and hamper you, or constrain you, or curtail you in any way. I know how hard-earned it is, how well deserved it is. You have your scars, too, Mel, but for all that I still want a new freedom.'

He paused, took a razor-edged breath. Then spoke again.

'I want the freedom to say this, Mel.' He took another breath, just as sharp, and absolutely vital to his existence. 'You said if I hadn't known about the baby we could have been free of each other.'

Between them, the silence stretched. Mel could not speak, could say nothing at all, for suddenly there was no breath in her lungs—no breath at all—and still the silence stretched between them.

Then... 'I don't want to be free of you.' Nikos's voice seared into the silence. 'When I saw that car hit you— oh, God, I thought you were dead. I thought you were *dead*! That I'd lost you for ever. And it was the worst moment of my life.'

It felt as if his heart was being impaled, speared again by the terror he'd felt as he'd watched her crumple to the ground. He relived that moment of absolute nightmare, knowing with grovelling gratitude to all the powers-that-be that he'd been spared. Knowing with a blaze in his head, in his heart, that he could not go on without speaking.

He surged on. It was too late to stop now—far, far too late.

'I want you to come back to me so much. I can't help hoping…hoping against hope…that despite everything—despite all that you've ever said to me—you might just—just…' He took a final ragged breath. 'Just want to come back to me. That you might just,' he said, and his eyes could not leave hers…not for a second, not for an instant, 'want to make your life with me.'

He had said it. Finally he had said it.

His heart was bared now, and it was beating for her and her alone. And if she spurned it—if she looked at him with pity, with rejection, after hearing words that had only made her want to flee from him the more—then he would bear it. But if he didn't put his words out there, then she might never know…never guess…just what he felt for her.

'I don't want to be free of you, Mel. I *can't* be free of you. You're in my head, and in my thoughts, and in my blood. You're in my *heart*, Mel…'

His eyes were blazing…the blood was roaring in his veins.

'There's only one freedom I want, Mel. I want to be free to love you.'

There was silence—absolute silence.

Nikos's gaze lasered down at her, willing her to speak. To say something—anything. But she simply lay there, her face as white as ice. Then he saw slow, thick tears start to ooze from beneath her eyelids.

He was at her side in an instant—a fraction of a second. Seizing her hands, clutching them to him.

'Mel! Don't cry—oh, my darling one, don't cry. I'm sorry—I'm sorry that I said all that to you. I should never have burdened you with it.'

But she only wept more, and he had to scoop his arm around her shoulders and cradle her against him. She wept into him—tears and tears and more tears. He soothed her hair and held her close, and closer still. And then, somewhere at his shoulder, he heard her speak. Muffled and tearful.

Carefully, mindful of how fragile her body was, he lowered her back upon the pillows. But she clung to his hand still. Her eyes swam with tears.

'I want that freedom, too. Oh, Nikos, I want it more than anything in the world!' Her face crumpled again. 'I want to be free to love you, free to *tell* you that I love you. And to love you the way I do.'

She wept again, and he held her again, and she was as light as a feather. For all the world weighed nothing now—nothing at all.

'I missed you so much,' she sobbed. 'I tried so hard not to miss you, but I did. All the time in America I missed you. I missed you wherever I went. Everywhere without you was...*awful*. I wanted you with me. On the Staten Island Ferry, at the top of the Empire State Building... I wanted to laugh with you in Las Vegas, revel in all its gaudy garishness. And I wanted you to stand beside me at the rim of the Grand Canyon and look down a mile deep into the earth. I wanted you everywhere I went. And you weren't there, Nikos, because

I'd walked out on you—and I'd walked out on you because…because…'

The sobbing came again, and once again he was
soothing her, stroking her hair, clasping her hand tight,
so tight.

'Because I knew that if I didn't go then, I'd never go.
And I *had* to go—it was a holiday romance we had—
only that. That was all you wanted—and all I wanted—
all I thought it would ever be. But it wasn't, Nikos—it
wasn't, it *wasn't*… But it had never been *supposed* to be
anything more than a holiday romance because I wanted
to be free—free like I've wanted to be for so, *so* long.'

She pulled away from him, her face working, full
of anguish.

'When I first found out I was pregnant I…I was
distraught. I was terrified that I'd be plunged back
into having to take care of another human being just
when I'd got my own life back. But at the same time
I felt my heart leap with joy. I had a *baby* growing inside me—a wondrous new life—and it was *your* baby,
Nikos. Yours. And I realised…I realised…' her eyes
were clinging to his and her hands were clinging to
him '…I realised, Nikos, that all I wanted on this earth
was to be free to love my baby—free to want my baby
more than anything else in all the world. And because
of that…because of that—'

She broke off, tears welling again, her voice choked
with emotion, with discovery.

'Because all I wanted was to love my baby I knew…I
knew—oh, Nikos—I knew it meant I was free to love.
Free to love *you*. Love you the way I wanted to. The way
I'd feared to because it was loving my poor grandfather
that kept me by his side so long. I feared love would be

a tie. And I thought all I wanted was to be free of all ties. Free of all bonds.'

Tears flowed down her cheeks and she felt her heart must surely overflow with the emotion now pouring through her.

'But to love *you*, Nikos, is to be free.'

He moved to sweep her to him, but she held him back, fear leaping in her eyes.

'But *am* I free to love you, Nikos? Am I? You talked of standing by me and "responsibilities". And—'

'Mel, my darling one, I said that only because I didn't want to burden you with my wanting you the way I do. With my wanting, more than anything in this life, to be your husband—your devoted, loving husband—the father to our beloved child—with you, my beloved wife.'

She gave a little choke of laughter and of tears. Of happiness and bliss.

'What fools we've been. Denying what we both craved.'

'Each other!' Nikos finished, and then he swept her to him, wanting no more pointless words, no more unnecessary doubts, no more fleeting fears.

He was free, finally, to hold her, to embrace her, to kiss her—to love her. As she was free to love him in return. And they were both free to love the child she carried.

Free to be happy with each other—all their lives.

A cough sounded from the doorway. They sprang apart. The nurse took in Mel's tear-stained face and frowned slightly.

'Happy tears or sad tears?' she asked enquiringly, with a lift of her eyebrow.

'Happy,' said Mel and Nikos in unison.

The nurse's gaze went to their fast-clasped hands,

and she nodded. 'Not too much emotion,' she advised, with another nod and a smile. 'Not good for baby.'

She picked up the notes from the foot of the bed, glancing at them. 'Overnight stay for observation,' she confirmed. Then she glanced at Nikos. 'I'm sorry to tell you this, but it's not actually visiting hours at the moment. It's only because your—'

'Wife-to-be,' Nikos inserted, throwing a glance at Mel.

'Your wife-to-be,' echoed the nurse dutifully, 'has come up here from A&E.' She looked again at the pair of them. 'It's visiting hours at six, so come back then. In the meantime...' her mouth twitched, and her expression was sympathetic now '...you've got five more minutes.' She whisked out.

Nikos turned to Mel. His heart was soaring. Soaring like a bird in flight.

'Will five minutes do it?' he asked her, his brow lifting questioningly.

Mel shook her head. She was floating somewhere above the surface of the hospital bed—she didn't know where. Didn't care.

Had it been so simple? Had a holiday romance been the real thing all along?

I wanted freedom, but my freedom is here—here with Nikos. Here with our child, waiting to be born.

She felt her heart constrict. Whatever names Nikos might want, one she knew. If their baby was a boy it would be named for her grandfather. The grandfather she had loved so much. Not the stricken husk he had become, but the loving, protective grandfather she remembered so clearly.

Oh, Gramps—you wanted me to find a good man— and now I have. I have!

'OK,' said Nikos. 'Well, if five minutes won't do it...' his eyes softened as he gazed down at her, the woman he had claimed the freedom to love '...how about fifty years?'

Her face lit. 'Sounds good to me,' she said. 'Sounds *very* good!'

He bent to kiss her. 'To our Golden Wedding Anniversary, then, and all the golden years between.'

'To our golden years together,' echoed Mel, and kissed him back.

EPILOGUE

THE CHRISTENING PARTY at Nikos and Mel's newly acquired family-sized villa on the coast outside Athens
was crowded with guests. Mel sat in almost regal splendour on the sofa, and young Nikos Stephanos Albert—
already known as Nicky—lay on her lap, resplendent
in his christening gown, fast asleep, oblivious to all the
admiring comments that came his way.

The vast majority of those came from his doting parents, and Nikos, standing beside the sofa, was gazing
down at his newborn son with an expression little short
of besotted, accepting all the homage as nothing more
than perfectly right and reasonable. Their son *was* the
most amazing baby ever, and no other could *possibly*
be even a fraction as wonderful.

They were not alone in this view, for Nikos's parents
shared it with them.

'Hah!' exclaimed Stephanos Parakis proudly, gazing
benignly down at his grandson.

'He looks like you,' said his wife fondly. His *new* wife.

Nikos's eyes tore themselves away from his infant
son and settled with approval on Adela Parakis. Even
if she hadn't turned out to be a very calm and level-
headed divorcee of forty-plus, rather than the sultry
mistress he'd assumed, Nikos would have approved of

her. For she had been the catalyst that had finally triggered his parents' decision to call time on their tormented marriage.

One of the catalysts, Nikos acknowledged.

The other was the elegant silver-haired man at the side of Nikos's mother—the new Principessa Falesi. The widowed Principe had met her at a party in Milan, and such had been his admiration for her that his mother had received with equanimity the news that her husband wished to remarry.

Now, as Principessa, she was enjoying a new lease of life—and of beauty. For as her son's eyes perused her they could see that his mother had clearly undergone a facelift, chosen a dramatically more flattering hairstyle and, if he were not mistaken, had a few additional discreet nips and tucks, as well.

He was glad for her—glad for both his parents. Glad for their late happiness with other partners, and glad that their respective remarriages had enabled them—finally—to be civil to each other…especially when they now had a common fascination with their grandson.

'He has my eyes,' observed the Principessa with complacent satisfaction, approaching with her new husband.

'He does,' Mel smiled. Nikos's mother was being very gracious towards her, and Mel wanted to keep her that way. So she didn't point out that *all* newborns had blue eyes.

Nikos refrained from telling his mother that, actually, his son had his wife's eyes—which just happened to be the most beautiful eyes in the world…

Memory struck through him—how Mel had flashed her sapphire eyes at him in that very first encounter, and how they had pierced him like Cupid's proverbial arrow.

Happiness drenched through him. And disbelief.

A holiday romance? How could he *ever* have been idiotic enough to think Mel—wonderful, fabulous, adorable, beloved Mel—could be nothing more than a holiday romance? She was the most precious person in the world to him.

Along with Nicky, of course.

Instinctively he lifted Mel's free hand in his and wound his fingers warmly into hers. She shifted her gaze to look at him, love shining in her eyes.

'A daughter next, I would recommend,' the Principessa said to Mel.

'Oh, yes,' agreed Mel. 'That would be ideal.'

'But you must watch your figure, my dear,' her mother-in-law reminded her.

'I fully intend to aspire to be as elegant as *you* in that respect,' Mel assured her, and nodded admiringly.

The Principessa gave a little laugh, and bestowed a careful smile of approval on her daughter-in-law. 'You must visit us in Milan, my dear, when my grandson is old enough to travel,' she said, catching her new husband's arm.

'Oh, that would be *lovely*!' enthused Mel. She glanced up at Nikos. 'Wouldn't it?'

'Yes, indeed,' he said hurriedly. 'Are you leaving already?' he asked.

'Alas, we must. We are flying home this evening.'

The guests were starting to disperse, and shortly after his mother's departure Nikos's father left as well, informing his son as he did so that Mel, Nicky and he were also invited to visit himself and Adela whenever they liked.

Nikos thanked him heartily, and saw them both to their car. As he came back into the villa Mel was in the hallway, cradling Nicky, who was now wide awake.

'He needs a change,' she said cheerfully. 'Want to help?'

'I wouldn't miss it for the world.' Nikos grinned. 'Do you mean a nappy-change? Or a change out of that metre-long silk embroidered concoction he's wearing?'

'Both,' said Mel. 'And then, if you won't think me a bad mother, I'll hand him over to Nanny, and you and I can sneak off to dinner before he needs his next feed.'

She gave a wry little smile of gratitude. It was amazing, she acknowledged, just how easy motherhood was when there was a nanny on hand. And when the baby's father was as devoted and willing as Nikos was.

'Great idea,' Nikos said with enthusiasm. 'It's more than time I had you to myself again.'

As they headed upstairs to the lavishly decorated suite that was Nicky's nursery Nikos said, 'By the way, we've been invited to a wedding—'

'Oh? Whose?' asked Mel interestedly.

Nikos gave a glinting smile. 'Would you believe Fiona Pellingham—and Sven?'

Mel gave her gurgle of laughter. 'His name's Magnus,' she said. 'But it's lovely news. I'm so glad for her.'

'Well, you were the matchmaker there,' Nikos reminded her.

Mel smiled fondly at her husband. 'And she was ours in a way, too, if you think about it. If she hadn't been pursuing you, you'd never have asked me out.'

Nikos put his arm around her shoulder. 'I'd have found another reason,' he answered. 'There was no way I could ever get you out of my head.'

She paused at the top of the stairs to kiss his cheek.

Her eyes were soft with love. 'Nor me you,' she assured him.

The dark eyes glinted with wicked humour. 'Love at first sight, was it?'

She spluttered, remembering their intemperate sparring at that first prickly encounter in the sandwich shop. 'We got all the aggro out of the way,' she told him firmly. 'Oh, and on the subject of sandwich shops—I heard that the Sarrie's Sarnies franchise is going great guns. Thanks to your business loan.'

'Well, didn't I promise that if his turnover increased I'd consider funding his expansion?' Nikos reminded her as they gained Nicky's bathroom and got to work on the delicate task of parting him from his ornate christening robe.

'He's very grateful,' Mel assured him. 'And so,' she added, 'is Joe. For sponsoring that new homeless shelter he's in, and the medics for addiction and alcoholism treatment.'

'Well, I'm grateful to Joe in return,' Nikos riposted. 'When I showered him with all those damn pound coins you'd dumped on me in your splenetic rage...' he ducked as Mel swung him a playful thump of objection, then lifted Nicky free of his gown '...I realised you were right about more than just how the booze was killing him—that you were *entitled* to be put out about the way I behaved to you. And that I owed you flowers to make amends.'

Mel gently laid their infant son down on his changing mat. 'Well,' she said, throwing another wicked glance at her husband, 'you can go on making amends.' She stepped aside. 'Go on—your turn for the nappy-change.'

'I couldn't just hand you the clean nappy, could I?' Nikos asked hopefully.

'Nope,' said his wife sternly.

Her husband dropped a resigned kiss on her forehead. 'It's a price I'll pay willingly for a happy marriage,' he told her.

Mel reached up to him with her mouth. 'Correction,' she told him. 'For the happiest marriage in the world.'

She took a wad of cotton wool, holding it at the ready for Nikos, talcum powder in her other hand.

Nikos grinned. 'Right, as always,' he agreed.

Then, with a squaring of his shoulders, he got to work to prove to the woman he loved just how much he loved her...

And beneath their joint ministrations the child who had brought them back together gazed cherubically up at the two people who loved only him more than they loved each other.

* * * * *

#3361 THE GREEK COMMANDS HIS MISTRESS
The Notorious Greeks
by Lynne Graham

Making billions and bedding women couldn't make Bastien Zikos forget the lustrous and defiant Delilah Moore. So Bastien has gone to great lengths to ensure that the one—*and only*—woman to have ever refused him returns to his bed!

#3362 BOUND TO THE WARRIOR KING
by Maisey Yates

Untamed Tarek al-Khalij was never meant to rule Tahar. More familiar with a sword than a crown, this warrior must now heal the suffering his brother's rule inflicted. To do it, he needs his most precious weapon yet...a royal bride!

#3363 TRADED TO THE DESERT SHEIKH
Scandalous Sheikh Brides
by Caitlin Crews

In the desert, Sheikh Kavian's word is law. So the defiance of his promised queen, Amaya, who flees after their betrothal ceremony, is intolerable! Kavian's already tasted her sweetness—perhaps his reluctant bride-to-be needs reminding of the pleasure *he* can give...

#3364 HER NINE MONTH CONFESSION
One Night With Consequences
by Kim Lawrence

The merest *glimpse* of handsome and sophisticated Benedict Warrender was enough to make wallflower Lily Gray blush. Until a twist of fate allows her to enter his orbit for one life-altering night...with consequences!

#3365 A PAWN IN THE PLAYBOY'S GAME
by Cathy Williams

Alessandro Falcone is notorious for winning in *every* pursuit. Being forced back to Scotland on business is an inconvenience for the billionaire bachelor—until the delectable Laura Reid becomes a welcome distraction on the long, cold Highland nights...

#3366 A BRIDE WORTH MILLIONS
by Chantelle Shaw

Innocent Athena Howard can't believe she escaped The Wedding of the Year only to fall *straight* into Luca De Rossi's arms! It must be fate. The cutthroat businessman needs a wife, and fast...will Athena accept his offer worth millions?

#3367 VOWS OF REVENGE
by Dani Collins

Melodie Parnell has always wanted to experience insatiable passion, and she thinks she's found it in Roman Killian's bed. But in the aftermath of their lovemaking, Melodie is catapulted back to reality when Roman reveals his true plans...to ruin her!

#3368 FROM ONE NIGHT TO WIFE
One Night With Consequences
by Rachael Thomas

Three months ago, Serena James had her heart broken by a man she'll never forget, especially not the fury in his eyes the night they parted. Now she's back in Santorini to tell him that their summer fling had unexpected repercussions...

REQUEST YOUR FREE BOOKS!

HARLEQUIN

Presents®

2 FREE NOVELS PLUS
2 FREE GIFTS!

PASSION
GUARANTEED
SEDUCTION

YES! Please send me 2 FREE Harlequin Presents® novels and my 2 FREE gifts (gifts are worth about $10). After receiving them, if I don't wish to receive any more books, I can return the shipping statement marked "cancel." If I don't cancel, I will receive 6 brand-new novels every month and be billed just $4.30 per book in the U.S. or $5.24 per book in Canada. That's a saving of at least 13% off the cover price! It's quite a bargain! Shipping and handling is just 50¢ per book in the U.S. and 75¢ per book in Canada.* I understand that accepting the 2 free books and gifts places me under no obligation to buy anything. I can always return a shipment and cancel at any time. Even if I never buy another book, the two free books and gifts are mine to keep forever.

106/306 HDN GHRP

Name	(PLEASE PRINT)

Address		Apt. #

City	State/Prov.	Zip/Postal Code

Signature (if under 18, a parent or guardian must sign)

Mail to the **Reader Service:**
IN U.S.A.: P.O. Box 1867, Buffalo, NY 14240-1867
IN CANADA: P.O. Box 609, Fort Erie, Ontario L2A 5X3

**Are you a current subscriber to Harlequin Presents® books
and want to receive the larger-print edition?
Call 1-800-873-8635 or visit www.ReaderService.com.**

* Terms and prices subject to change without notice. Prices do not include applicable taxes. Sales tax applicable in N.Y. Canadian residents will be charged applicable taxes. Offer not valid in Quebec. This offer is limited to one order per household. Not valid for current subscribers to Harlequin Presents books. All orders subject to credit approval. Credit or debit balances in a customer's account(s) may be offset by any other outstanding balance owed by or to the customer. Please allow 4 to 6 weeks for delivery. Offer available while quantities last.

Your Privacy—The Reader Service is committed to protecting your privacy. Our Privacy Policy is available online at www.ReaderService.com or upon request from the Reader Service.

We make a portion of our mailing list available to reputable third parties that offer products we believe may interest you. If you prefer that we not exchange your name with third parties, or if you wish to clarify or modify your communication preferences, please visit us at www.ReaderService.com/consumerschoice or write to us at Reader Service Preference Service, P.O. Box 9062, Buffalo, NY 14240-9062. Include your complete name and address.

HP15

SPECIAL EXCERPT FROM

 HARLEQUIN

Presents

One night...one secret that will change everything!
What will Benedict Warrender do when he
discovers the truth?

Read on for a sneak preview of
HER NINE MONTH CONFESSION,
the latest book from the fabulous
Kim Lawrence

Behind Lily the water appeared clear azure, blending almost seamlessly into the sky. Ahead of her it was turquoise and clear as crystal. The warmth was totally seductive and though she had only intended to stay out for a few minutes she had quickly lost track of time. She was enjoying swimming lazily, though she kept in mind the maid's story of the tourist who, after a boozy dinner, had ignored the warning signs or probably had not seen them and tragically drowned because he'd ventured past the protective reef.

One of the things she had noticed about motherhood was it made a person very aware of their own mortality and a lot more risk averse. Not that she'd ever been a massive risk taker—well, only once!

Seeing the shore through a watery haze and pretty much spent, Lily paused and, holding her chin up, felt for the sandy bottom, acknowledging the toe contact with a sigh of relief. She bounced along for a few feet, spitting out water before she could place her feet flat on the sand.

With the water at shoulder level she walked her way down to waist level, aware as she did so that she wasn't alone. There was a figure on the beach.

She assumed it was one of her fellow guests. This stretch of beach, though not private, was, because of its remote inaccessibility, used almost exclusively by the guests at the beach resort. Lily lifted one hand in greeting while she pushed her wet hair back from her face with the other and blinked away the water from her eyelashes.

Then her vision cleared.

For a moment shock wiped her mind as she refused to accept what she was seeing. Her heart thudding with adrenaline-fuelled speed, she closed her eyes, wiped away the moisture with her hand and opened them again.

He was still there, the man in the incongruous dark suit, tall, dark and terrifyingly familiar. He returned her stare with incredible eyes, the colour rare but not unique—she saw that colour every day.

The last time she'd looked into those eyes she had melted. She didn't melt now—she froze. Every muscle and nerve fibre went into shock. Her brain shut down, a protective response to a situation where she had no other defenses to fall back on.

HARLEQUIN

Presents®

This month, read the fabulous conclusion to
Lynne Graham's latest duet, *The Notorious Greeks*,
a story packed full of fiery passion, impossible
temptation and a love that just won't be denied!

"I always get what I want…and I want you."

Nothing has made Bastien Zikos forget the lustrous
dark hair, haunting eyes and outrageous defiance of
Delilah Moore. And he's gone to great lengths to ensure
that the one—*and only*—woman to have ever turned
him down returns to him.

If Delilah wants to save her father's ailing business,
she must agree to Bastien's commands: be his mistress,
wear his diamonds and wait for him in his bed!

Find out what happens next in:

THE GREEK COMMANDS
HIS MISTRESS

September 2015